D0113718

FIRST VOYAGE OUT

Charles M. Kenyon

FOUR WINDS PRESS • NEW YORK

Published by Four Winds Press, a division of Scholastic Magazines, Inc., New York, N.Y.
Library of Congress Catalog Card No.: 67-23542

FIRST
VOYAGE
OUT

Chapter
1

The year was 1841. The day was bright and cloudless, such as come to Rhode Island in late summer. In the pocket-sized potato field stretched out between the granite rocks a powerfully built, shirtless young man was chopping out ragweed for the last time.

At the far edge of the field a gravel road, long and straight across the marshes, shimmered in the afternoon heat. Clumps of beach plum and bayberry bushes lined the road, here blotting out whole sections, there just nibbling a bit from the sides.

Down the road from behind one of these clumps of bushes a man's figure came into view, and Nat Goodwin leaned on his hoe for a moment to watch him approach.

A canvas bag was slung over the man's shoulder. Apparently it weighed little for it rode easily on the round back. He was a small man, but he walked with long strides, his head bobbing forward and back, much like a chicken's, with each step. His trousers were rolled up almost to his knees, after the fashion of sailors swabbing decks. His striped jersey flapped loosely around his thin chest.

As he reached the far corner of Nat's field, he left the road and came directly toward the boy. He gave no sign of recognition until he was two strides away. Then he stopped and peered closely into Nat's face.

It was a broad face with prominent cheekbones and widely spaced gray eyes beneath eyebrows that made a straight line from end to end. Although he had no beard yet, the afternoon sun glinted on the fuzz that was sprouting on his square and solid jaw. Above the forehead, studded now with beads of sweat, a mop of sun-bleached hair curled in the wind. He had a short, broad snub nose that turned up a bit on the end and was heavily freckled across the bridge. But it was the boy's eyes that held Manuel's attention — steady, clear, probing, they showed the understanding of a mature intelligent man.

"You're him," Manuel said at last, nodding his head quickly to affirm his statement. "You're Goodwin."

"I'm Nat Goodwin," the boy agreed, searching the man's face for a clue to recognition.

"Nat. Nat Goodwin. That's the name. You're his son." The swarthy face nodded up and down again. "I come all this way to see you and your mother."

"What about?"

"Name's Bella. They call me Manuel. Where's your mother?" Manuel's leathery face squeezed up into a look of concern. "Is she still alive?"

"She is." Nat turned toward the house; without another word passing between them the muscular boy and the little man strode across the field.

Mrs. Goodwin, considered a widow by the townsfolk since her husband had been reported lost on the return of the whaler *Mingo Chief* three years before, was a plump, ruddy woman obviously quite capable of taking care of herself. She was sitting under the apple tree by the kitchen door. Her reddish-brown hair was drawn smoothly back and knotted low on her neck. She wore a loose-fitting cotton dress gathered tightly at the wrists and held at the throat with an intricately carved whalebone pin.

"Mother," said Nat. "This is Manuel Bella. He wants to speak with us. I think it's about Father."

The long curling peel from the early yellow apple she was paring hung motionless, then broke and fell into the bowl on her lap. "What is it, Mr. Bella?" Mrs. Goodwin looked him squarely in the face, her blue eyes appraising him shrewdly. "Do you have news?"

"No news." Manuel shook his head. "No news, Mrs. Goodwin. But I think he's still alive."

Nat waited for Manuel to continue, but the little man remained silent. Nat's memory leaped back five long years to a day he and his father had been sitting beside the same potato patch Nat hoed so short a time ago. They sat side by side on a rough bench made by rolling a log up to the stone wall. Too big to sit on his father's lap, yet too young not to want to, Nat pressed close to his father's side. His small legs stretched straight out in front of him in miniature imitation of his father's long ones.

He wriggled his toes in the sun, happy because he was

close to his father and proud because his father was talking to him as though he were a man.

His father was telling again about how he had gone to sea when he was a boy after his own father had been killed in the famous battle between the *Constitution* and the *Guerrière*. How he had met Nat's mother, married her, and settled down in Little Compton.

"But I'm not much as a farmer, Nat, and I've a chance to try again for a bit of the greasy luck before I'm too old. A good cruise would give me enough to be sure of your schoolin', lad, and enough to improve our way of livin' a bit too."

Nat didn't believe that he wanted their way of living changed much. Their house was snug and warm, his mother's cooking satisfied him, and beyond hoping for a guarantee of sunny days on Saturdays he'd leave life as it was. But to keep his father happy, he nodded agreement. He had complete faith that his father would do the right thing.

"Second mate's not a bad berth for me, so long from the sea, and Jabez Collins says they need a steady man to keep the crew in shape this cruise."

"But how do you know you'll get the job, Pa, specially if it's such a good one?"

His father hesitated before answering. "I'm a lucky man, Nat. Things usually work for me if I want 'em to badly enough. You'll probably be lucky too. Some men are and some aren't and that's a fact. . . . And besides, the captain on this *Mingo Chief* is supposed to be a real Tartar. There's quite a few won't sail with him though he always brings back oil." He shrugged. "I know little about him, but time will change that soon enough."

His father reached out and took Nat's hand, a look of concern in his gray eyes. "I'll be missing you, lad, and when I set eyes on you next you'll be a man. You've been a good son, Nat, and if you follow your conscience, you'll be a good man too."

The sound of his mother's voice cut through Nat's reverie.

"Explain yourself, Mr. Bella."

"Well," began Manuel, "there ain't much to explain. I and Mr. Goodwin and John Scotsen and Jacob whose other name I forget was a working party for wood in the Gilbert Islands. Suddenly we was jumped by a bunch of cannibals and Mr. Goodwin was further from the boat than most. The captain, he was ashore with us, and he shoved off, leaving Mr. Goodwin. The cannibals caught him all right and Captain Bradner says they cut off his head on the spot. Beggin' your pardon, ma'am, for the gory details. But me, I thought they whacked him one with a club which could have just knocked him out.

"The captain put it in the log that he was beheaded by savages, and that was that. He hated Mr. Goodwin something terrible. They was most unlike, ma'am. The captain's uncommon cruel and real greedy — most greedy I've ever heard about — and a lot of us thought . . ."

Mrs. Goodwin firmly pulled him back to the subject. "Wouldn't Mr. Goodwin be dead by now if the savages had captured him?"

Nat reached out and took his mother's hand. Its shaking betrayed her calm face. Her hand firmed in his grasp, however, and gave him a squeeze of assurance. His mother had never been one to shirk her responsibilities, and she had always taught Nat that he must learn to face facts if he were ever to become a real man.

Here she sat, facing widowhood in her mid-thirties, a lonely path of hard years lying before her. With her emotions well under control, she asked not for idle hopes but for the truth.

"We must learn the facts, Nat. If Mr. Bella has facts, that's one thing. But if he hasn't, let's not build a dream world about us. Proceed, Mr. Bella."

"Sometimes these savages just keep a man as a slave." Manuel's face was twitching under the unaccustomed strain of being the center of attention. "Now my last voyage out I met a whaleman in Santiago. He was in from around the islands and he said that the Kanakas spoke of a big white man with blond hair kept as a slave in the Gilberts."

"It's Father!" Nat leaped to his feet with excitement. "We must save him. He's alive. I've felt it all along."

His mother's steady tone cut him short. "Where in Santiago did you meet this sailor? In a grog shop?"

"Yes, ma'am." Manuel dropped his gaze.

"Was he drunk?"

"Yes, ma'am."

"How about you?"

"Yes, ma'am, but not too drunk to remember. His name was Albert Varney and he said the Kanaka who told him about the white prisoner was Joe Papeete, a good boy."

Mrs. Goodwin sighed. "It's not much of a story, Nat. A drunken sailor got it from another drunken sailor who got it from a pagan savage — probably drunk too." For several seconds Mrs. Goodwin sat looking into the distance above the tops of the wood-lot trees. As the fingers of her left hand played with the hem of her apron, her gold wedding ring gleamed in the sun. She shifted her gaze back to Nat's eager face, but her own eyes held only sympathy and understanding, not hope.

But Nat turned eagerly toward Bella. "Did you tell this story to the authorities?"

"I told Captain Bradner, but he wasn't likely to do anything about it. He won't never admit he's wrong on anything. But I know more than to think he's always right! Sometimes *I'm* right. An' the Navy's got a sloop out there now could help us, but the captain said don't go tellin' tales to them or he'd have me flayed in the riggin'."

Suddenly looking tired, Mrs. Goodwin picked up the apple she'd been paring when Manuel Bella arrived. "I guess that's all."

"Except this," added Manuel, rummaging deep into his sea bag. "My drinkin' friend in Santiago got it from the Kanaka . . . a *Christian* Kanaka," he added with deep emphasis. He held out a crude statue about four inches high of a pagan god seated cross-legged, his eyes closed, patiently waiting. Manuel's skinny finger pointed to the bottom. Carved deeply into the base was "N-G-1840."

Nat took the statue from Manuel's hand and silently turned it over and over. Finally he spoke, his young voice shaking. "I'm going, Mother. Father is alive."

His mother shook her head. "It's not much to go on, Nat. A thin tale doesn't become true even when it's backed up by a piece of whittling. You'd best stay home."

She turned to Manuel and said, "You've come a long

way, and we're grateful. We hope you'll stay the night before starting back."

Manuel nodded. In his simple mind he had completed his task. He had brought word to the family. Now he could relax. The decisions were someone else's to make. But the thought of a soft bed and a good meal pleased him, because in his life he had seldom either one. "Thank you, ma'am," he mumbled.

Though the news Manuel brought did not convince Mrs. Goodwin, it fired Nat. He *knew* that his father was alive. He *knew* that he could rescue him. And as he picked up his tools and returned them to the shed his imagination began to work on how the rescue could be accomplished. As he tossed cracked corn to the chickens, the chicken-yard fence became a prisoners' stockade. Before he dumped them into the battered wood box by the black kitchen stove, the chunks of firewood in his arms became weapons of combat. While the bucket creaked its slow way upward with clear water for their suppers, the windlass over the well became a device for hoisting a man to freedom.

When Nat looked at the supper table set for three instead of the accustomed two, he thought of his father, his mother, and himself. And when his mother called them to the table, he went directly to his father's seat and motioned Manuel to the one he himself had sat in since he was big enough to sit.

Throughout the meal Nat plied the Portuguese with questions about the South Seas, about the ship, about whales — his excitement increasing by the moment. But Mrs. Goodwin, busy with her own thoughts, had little to say. Her plump, sturdy figure moved efficiently around the kitchen, quickly disposing of the various chores meal-time means to women. As she cleared away the soup bowls which had held the thick suppertime stew and slipped the stewed pears and soft, fat molasses cookies in front of them, she broke abruptly into their conversation.

"Mr. Bella, do you have any plans in mind . . . if Mr. Goodwin is down there?"

Manuel's dark eyes eloquently showed his sadness. "Ma'am, since I was a little boy I can't think much. And mostly people don't believe me much. But God won't let me sleep easy if I don't get help to him. No one up here can do anything. Someone down there in the islands might. I tried an' I can't." He put a spoonful of pears into his mouth. Mrs. Goodwin glanced at Nat.

"He's right, Mother. We can't do anything way up here."

"And how do you propose to get down there?"

Manuel gulped down his pears and pointed at Nat with his spoon. "He's big enough," he said. "The *Mingo Chief* is in Bristol lookin' for seamen. That's where I come from. Maybe they'd sign him on, I think."

Nat waited for his mother to speak. She sighed, and dropped her hand lightly on Nat's shoulder. "How soon would you have to leave?"

"Soon as we can. Ship sails day after tomorrow."

"I'll get my sewing box," Mrs. Goodwin said brusquely. "There's a lot of sewing to be done. You two get at the dishes."

In the morning Nat started down the long road which would lead him to Bristol and the wharf where the *Mingo*

Chief was signing on a crew for the long voyage to the South Pacific.

Over his shoulder was a bag like Manuel's full of clothing which his mother had spent all night in making ready. At the bend beyond the potato patch, Nat turned to look back. His mother waved from the door, and he waved in return. He would not see her again for many years. Tears brimmed in his eyes.

"Let 'em fall," said Manuel at his side. "The's nothin' wrong with a man cryin' a bit when he ought to."

Chapter
2

THE BLUE WATERS of Narragansett Bay shimmered in the distance. As the road topped a rocky knoll, Nat saw the needle-thin masts and spars of a ship in the distance. He pointed. "Yonder's Bristol Harbor, I guess, Manuel."

Manuel shaded his eyes with a skinny brown hand. "That's the direction, but your eyes must be better'n mine. You'll be a good lookout." Winded by the long gradual climb, they let their burdens fall to the ground and sat on a granite outcropping.

"Manuel, what's whaling really like? . . . I mean, is it hard to learn . . . is it, well, do you think I'll be able to do it all right?"

"I do. I was littler than you, an' dumber too, an' I stayed alive at it. When I was a kid, I lived in the Azores. We was richer than most families. We owned a house, had a garden and goats. We didn't have any money, but we ate regular. An' that's more than a lot of my friends did. But there was too many of us — ten, eleven, I forget. An' no work. So when I was maybe fourteen my father says, 'Feed yourself, Manuel. You're big now.' Still no work on the island, so when one whaler comes in, the *Jupiter*, an' fever hit his crew, he signs me on. Them with fever got dumped ashore, an' away we sail. I been at it ever since."

"Was it hard getting used to living on the ship?"

"Was it hard! You bet! When you're little an' can't speak English! Oh boy!" Manuel shook his head, but he smiled, feeling the satisfaction a man has when he recalls a hard time he has come through successfully.

"How about the jobs you did?" Nat asked, grateful that he could speak English and that he was five-eleven and a hundred-and-eighty pounds.

"Jobs is what you make them," Manuel philosophized. "I did what they tol' me to as fast as I could. Then I got the fever. I pulled through all right, but they say that's why I ain't so good at thinkin' now. . . . Some things I never could learn, so I don't try."

"Don't you get dizzy way up in the rigging? When I'm up a high tree, I have to fight to keep from falling out. And once when I was smaller, I tumbled right off the ridge pole of our barn and Father caught me just as I was sliding off onto the ground."

"You hang on and pay attention to your work, there's no time to get dizzy." Manuel was trying hard to offer helpful advice. To a man who has spent most of his life at sea, however, the ways of the seaman were not at all strange. "You don't get seasick more than once, twice, three times maybe. You'll see. Next year this time you'll know the answers. All whalers learn 'em."

Changing the subject abruptly Nat asked, "What's this Captain Bradner like, Manuel? Is he a bad one?"

Manuel took his usual moment to collect his thoughts, his Adam's apple bobbing up and down in his thin neck while he swallowed.

"He does bad things an' he does good things. He knows whales better'n anyone. He makes the cook feed us good. His ship's a clean one." He drew his dark eyebrows together and swallowed again. "He's a cruel man an' he hates deserters. He shoots 'em. I've seen him."

"But that's murder, Manuel," said Nat, only half-believing what he heard.

"Not when you sign, boy, the law makes the captain be president, king, and all the judges. He's it. You won't forget that, I bet you! When Mr. Goodwin was aboard things weren't bad, most things didn't get the captain so upset because Mr. Goodwin took care of them. He was real fair to everybody. You got what was comin' to you good or bad, but you knew it was fair. . . ."

"Yes," said Nat, intending to stop the praise of his father because he had already heard it a dozen times over on the road from home. The little man certainly had a deep loyalty to Mr. Goodwin, so deep that Nat was sure Manuel would risk his life to rescue him.

Suddenly Manuel rose, slinging his bag to his shoulder. "Come on, lad, we can't put off life by sitting here. The ship you see is probably the *Mingo Chief*." He sighed and strode forward.

Nat trotted a few steps to catch up, then almost froze in mid-air. He heard the lethal buzz just as he saw the rattler directly in front of him. Before he even had time to think, a knife pinned the triangular head to the ground and the ugly coils twitched and writhed in their death struggle.

Manuel put his heel on the flat head, and deftly retrieved his thin, flat-handled knife. He jumped back, quickly wiped the blade with a bunch of brown tuft grass and slipped it into a canvas sheath.

"A little man don't have much chance some places," Manuel said gravely. "But with my little helper here I'm over six feet tall."

"I'd rather be with you than against you," said Nat dryly. "And thanks."

"You'll be needin' all the help you can get before you're home again. I'll teach you how to throw one. It might come in handy."

When Nat again saw the *Mingo Chief*, some of her sails were already fluttering in the crisp September breeze. Except for a couple of loungers standing by to cast off, and a young wife or two fluttering handkerchiefs, the wharf was deserted.

The ship was tied, bow downstream, to the end of a great stone quay which jutted into the bay for a hundred feet or more. The quay was two rectangular walls of square-cut granite blocks, each about a yard thick; the middle was filled in with gravel to make a roadbed.

The ship herself was a bluff-bowed, broad-beamed affair, with little of the grace Nat had imagined a ship would have. The thing about her which impressed him most was the rigging. Far above the deck towered a snarl of ropes and a tangle of sticks. The thought of climbing high into that spider web, even with the whaler steady at the dock, gave Nat a queasy feeling.

Nat took a tighter grip on his sea bag and stepped onto

the quay, still curiously eyeing the strange ship which loomed ahead like the wall of some incongruous wooden prison.

Looking down at him over the black rail high above was a huge brown-skinned man with a startling mane of straight, black hair. When Nat looked up, the man frowned deeply, and Nat's heart skipped a beat. Partly to cover his feelings, Nat smiled and waved to the savage above him. The frown faded, and the great face cracked into a grin. A giant arm waved in answering salute. Then the man walked quickly away from the rail.

Scarred and dented from stem to stern, the ship was obviously a veteran campaigner. But the bowsprit glistened new and clean, replacing one judged unseaworthy even by her parsimonious New England owners. Two new whaleboats swung from their davits, and forward on the same side was a third whaleboat, covered with fresh white paint that didn't begin to camouflage the buffets of battle. The rest of the ship was old, and looked it.

Along the black side ran a white band pierced at regular intervals by nine black squares. Yet even this decorative touch was functional. In faraway waters cannibals and coast-of-Asia pirates knew the might of British warships. The shrewd whalers had learned that neither of these adversaries would be so foolish as to come close enough to find out whether the ship was merely painted or, like the British frigates, had real gun ports which would suddenly open up to belch shot and flame at them.

Whaling was a deadly serious business — a hard life lacking many of the "necessities" people couldn't live without ashore. Seldom did a whaler end a voyage with the full crew, alive and unharmed, which had sailed with it three years before.

Disease took many lives; the men ate poorly, drank brackish water, and froze in the icy blasts of the Bering Sea or sweat their blood thin under the tropic sun. At this time many seamen had been imprisoned by the governors of ports in Chile and Peru on flimsy pretexts. Cannibals could, and did, overpower the crews of smaller boats. The ship itself devoured men like the Moloch of Judah. The rigging was undoubtedly picturesque, but a man could easily lose his footing on the slim rope which was his only platform while he worked with the slapping, bucking, billowing canvas perhaps eighty feet above the deck. A single slip and he hit the deck — or missed it — and the captain would be looking for another new hand at the next port of call.

Fingers mashed in blocks, legs caught in the coils of running rope, heads bashed in falls on the slippery decks and companionways, arms burned from the the tryworks as a ship boiled down in a rolling sea, bodies cut and gashed by the razor-sharp tools of the trade — these were the commonplace scars of their everyday life.

Men put up with all these dangers to go whaling. Some went because ambition drove them to try for the high stakes they might win; some whalers just drifted into whaling, as they drift into any trade, drift through their lives, and then disappear; some took their first cruise because work was hard to find and this was a living; some were "getting away" — boys running from farm life, men escaping the law or a nagging wife.

Nat's reason was his own. He was not yet excited by the thought of hunting the world's greatest animal, thrilled by dreams of faraway places, or drawn by the call of the sea. If he had his "druthers," he'd be back on their farm helping his mother. But he had a job to do. And if finding his father meant going aboard this floating barn, then get aboard he would. He trudged up the gangplank and, stepping down onto the oil darkened deck, resolutely left his own world behind him.

The decision was more fateful than Nat himself would have guessed. When his foot hit the gangplank he had left the world of the farmer forever behind. In the one-room school he had attended during the winter months he had liked arithmetic and was good at it, and the year around Nat and his mother both read books of all kinds. Nat enjoyed this stretching of his mind, but something inside him rebelled whenever his mother hinted that he might become a teacher, or even more when Parson Brown suggested the ministry to him. Yet he didn't really take to farming either. He farmed pretty well because he was strong and intelligent and conscientious. But he found no pleasure in the work either with the animals, as his cousin Abner did, or even bringing in a good harvest in the fall. It remained just work. But he knew no other life.

Captain Bradner was watching the mate check in a few last-minute supplies. He sat just forward of the main mast at a desk improvised by laying a plank across two kegs. He paid no attention at all to Manuel and Nat as they came aboard.

A very broad-shouldered man with a small head and a thin sunken face, the captain wore no hat, and his close-cropped hair glinted red in the sun. Although the day was warm, he wore a pea jacket buttoned up to the throat.

Emaciated hands protruded from the sleeves. As Nat approached, he saw the captain shudder.

Manuel was the first to speak.

"Captain, this man wants to sign on." The captain shifted his attention to Nat. As the thin, hawk-nosed face turned up to him, Nat gazed down into cold gray eyes. There was no flicker of interest in them, no sign of human warmth, no little creases about the corners to show that the face ever smiled. Below the nose, a lipless slit opened.

"What's your name?"

"Nat Goodwin, sir."

"You're a fool, Goodwin. You can't catch whales. You can't row a boat. You don't know a royal from a mainbrace or a gaff from a blubber pike. . . ." The captain's eyes searched Nat's face. "Goodwin," he repeated softly almost to himself. "Goodwin from Rhode Island. . . . You look like him, boy."

"Yes, sir," said Nat. "I do."

"He's dead," said the captain flatly. His voice began to rise again. "And you're a fool, boy. You know nothing . . . you farmer . . . except to hoe potatoes. Go back to that. I need a sailor. . . . But I don't want responsibility for you!" Abruptly he turned his attention to his papers.

Nat said nothing. His face slowly turned bright red and his muscles grew tense. For a few uncertain moments Nat simply stood still, unable to believe that he had been turned down so abruptly, not even sure that this was the end. But Nat was a tough Yankee, determined and stubborn about something as important to him as getting this job.

"Captain Bradner." The red head showed no sign of having heard. Nat raised his voice.

"Captain Bradner."

"I heard you the first time!" The captain set down his fistful of papers and rose slowly, almost stiffly, to his feet. Six-feet-four, with shoulders broad as a barn door, he towered above Nat. Yet he was not so much a giant as a great gaunt scarecrow of a man.

"I've told you once — and I told you kindly — *get out of here*. Now what keeps you?"

"Today I walked fourteen miles, Captain Bradner, to sign aboard your ship. I'm strong and healthy and willing to work. . . ."

"Willing ain't always enough, lad. What bloody thing can you do to earn your keep? Can you cook? Can you make barrels? Can you sew canvas? Can you stand a trick at the wheel?" The questions came so fast that Nat had no time to answer.

"Answer me!" roared the captain. "Are you any damned use at all?" As Nat started to speak, the captain bellowed again. "Do you know what a head spade is? . . . Answer me!"

"I don't know," replied Nat.

"A bone spade?"

"I don't know."

"A boarding knife?"

"I don't know."

"Can you slice bible leaves? . . . Answer me!"

"No, sir."

"What's a toggle iron?"

"I don't know."

"A cuddy board?"

"I don't know."

"A lion's tongue?"

"I don't know."

Abruptly the catechism stopped. "And you expect me to pay you wages. A useless know-nothing like you." Nat was being browbeaten and he knew it. But he didn't know how to get out from under. His frustration kindled his temper.

"I don't expect any more than the wages commonly paid beginners," he snapped. The captain was going to strike him. A voice at his right told him that Manuel had moved up beside him.

"The boy is strong, Captain," he said in his soft voice. "And we don't have all hands." The captain's gaze shifted slowly from Nat to the little Portuguese. Manuel pleaded and his head jerked in nervousness. An ordinary seaman didn't often stand up to his captain. A vibrant bass voice sliced the tense air.

"Cap'n, I like you take this one boy." It was the big Kanaka Nat had smiled a greeting to as they came aboard.

The captain started to shake his head. The incredibly deep voice continued.

"We sail many time, Cap'n. I no sign papers, you no ask me sign. Dis one boy sign, you get two men. One know-nothin', him. One know-ever't'ing, me." He smiled a friendly, guileless smile and added, "Man say *Niantic* need boat-steerer. What you t'ink?"

The captain's acid face suddenly smiled back at the big brown man. It was a smile so warm and friendly that the change left Nat stunned. And as long as he knew Captain Bradner, Nat could never decide whether the captain

signed him on because of Buck's threat to leave or through
a real liking for the big native.

"Think you can make a whaler out of this clodhopper,
hey?"

"I kin," said Buck solemnly. "Dis one's father made d'
best out o' me."

"Well, you make a whaler out of him. . . . And, Buck,
teach him what happens to men who jump ship. Don't let
him out of your sight. D' you hear?"

Nat signed on for one two-hundred-and-fiftieth of any
profits, just the same as a cabin boy. But his reason for
signing with this ship for this voyage was not to get rich.

He hoisted his sea bag to his shoulder and followed
Manuel forward.

Still blinded by the bright sunlight, he groped his way
into the murk of the tiny forecastle. Under Manuel's direction, he found his bunk with no trouble. A lopsided box
hung on the wall, broad toward the bows, almost coming
to a point at the other end; the bunk was little more than
five feet long. The bottom, bare of mattress or ticking, was
plain, hard board.

With a wry grin, he recalled that his mother always
said things could be worse. Maybe they could. Instead of
boards it could be slabs, round side up. Eyes more accustomed to the gloom he looked again, and with a sigh ran
his hand over the curved surface of slabs.

He changed quickly into old breeches and a knit shirt.
He carefully folded his best suit and laid it away in the
bottom of his bag. He moved slowly as he folded the
soft wool in his bony hands, and like a little boy rubbed it
against his cheek. The suit meant a great deal to him. It
was the first and only one he had ever owned. One day in

the general store while shopping with his mother, Nat had seen this bolt of wool cloth lying on the counter. A soft, brown herringbone weave, it seemed the finest cloth in the world. His mother, sensing what was in her son's mind, had said, "Nat, isn't it beautiful — but it's a dollar a yard. That's for rich people." And she'd laughed. Knowing that there was no money like that in his house, Nat had choked back his desire. But every time he came into the store he sneaked a look at that bolt of cloth still on the shelf. One Saturday it was gone.

When his birthday came around, he found out where it had gone. His mother had taken in sewing for townspeople all winter long until she finally had enough cash to buy the cloth and make it into a suit for him. Big for his years now, and still growing, he thought he might never put it on again. But he would remember it all his life.

Back on deck he went directly to the mate Manuel pointed out to him. Mr. Flanders was a short, stocky man with curly red hair and long sideburns. Rather a dandy ashore, Nat guessed, but all his attention was directed now to setting sail on the foremast.

"So you're Goodwin," he said curiously as Nat reported.

Nat grinned. "I guess everyone aboard knows that I don't know a thing about whaling. But I want to learn."

"Then learn to say 'sir' to officers aboard this ship," snapped Mr. Flanders. "That's your first lesson. And for your second, you'll get up there." He pointed in the general direction of the fore-topmast. "Up you go. Get next to Thurston. He'll tell you what to do."

Although not a sailor, Nat was strong and active. He easily grasped the shrouds and got his feet on the ratlines. The tarred line stuck comfortingly to his bare feet, and the slight give to his ladder aloft was not enough to concern him. Quickly he went up to the foretop. "Where's Thurston?" he shouted to a man balancing surely on a foot rope beneath the main yard.

"Topgallant yard," replied the other without looking up from his work. Nat looked up higher and higher into the rigging. He could see men's feet and legs beneath each of the yards; some still seemed a hundred feet above him. His confidence began to slip, but he took a deep breath and climbed higher. Although he knew better than to look down, by the time he had reached the fore-topsail yard, his old fear of height had returned, and his grip was losing its strength. Still above him he could see one man working alone on the fore-topgallant sail. He didn't think he could ever reach his post beside him, but somehow he did. Green with unreasoning fear, beaded with drops of cold sweat, he finally swung his toes over onto the horse and clutched the topgallant yard with both hands.

"Relax," said Thurston sardonically. "No one's ever fallen from here — twice."

Nat tried to grin, but no grin came. He looked down. Far below him he saw the white circle of Flander's face. The deck was a sliver of wood not so large as his own foot beneath him. While below he had noticed no motion at all, high on the tall mast he found there was a gentle swaying roll from side to side, enough, it seemed, to put him first over the starboard rail and then over the larboard.

"Farmer, hey!" Thurston said contemptuously. "Well you'd better get used to it. You're here for two years, an' nary a furrow to plow or a cow shed to clean. Loose all those lashings on the other side of the mast. We'll be setting this sail as soon as we clear the harbor."

Gripping whatever came close to hand with all the strength he could muster, Nat somehow made his way to the larboard foot rope, or "horse" as he soon learned to call it. With fumbling fingers he worked the sail lashings free to the end of the yard. Thurston was watching him closely. As soon as he finished, he was on him.

"And now, bucko, up to the royals with you. Same job." Nat hesitated, waiting for Thurston to start up. Thurston sneered. "Get started, my bucko, you go it alone." He grabbed a back stay with one hand, swung a leg around it and slid for the deck.

Watching him grow smaller and smaller, Nat felt a great wave of dizziness rise in him. He fought it down and started the terrible climb toward the crosstrees. Clinging at last to the royal yard he noticed a sliver of black opening up between the hull and the wharf. Quickly it broadened. Nat realized his cruise had begun. They were under way.

Captain Bradner skillfully put the sturdy ship out of the harbor under skeleton sail, clearing Hog Island, then the entire crew turned to until all sails were filled. An hour later with Brenton Point astern, the course was set for the Cape Verde Islands, three thousand miles away.

Chapter
3

NAT SPENT most of his time on deck because the tiny forecastle was always stuffy and crowded. The men below spent most of their time either sleeping or talking. And most of the talk, it seemed to Nat, was either boasting or endless argument about things none of the men knew anything about.

Furthermore, Nat stayed topsides because he had already developed a liking for the sea. He enjoyed the smell of the salt air in his nostrils and the sea wind blowing through his hair. He liked walking about the decks familiarizing himself with the parts and paraphernalia of the ship.

And at night he found the same stars his father had pointed out to him as a boy in their familiar places in the sky. When his father was at sea, Nat and Mrs. Goodwin often walked to the top of the knoll behind the house, and there Nat would proudly recite the names of the stars and the constellations. He had favorites — the Big Dipper, Cassiopeia, and the Seven Sisters (which he thought should be nine because that's how many he could see). Orion's Belt was always easy to find, and he could see Aldebaran, "the rider on the horse's back," in the handle of the Big Dipper. He and his mother would laugh about Betelgeuse, which in New England was called "Beetle Juice."

It was at night, too, that he felt most homesick and alone. Big as he was, he had never spent a night away from his own house until he joined the ship. Manuel was a friend, but not a close one. He was not in Nat's watch to begin with, and he was as old as Nat's father. Like the other foremast hands, he knew surprisingly little and cared less about the ship or the sea beyond his own tasks. Nat wanted to learn more.

Finally he went to Mr. Flanders, the pock-marked, fiery first mate, and borrowed a book on navigation by Nathaniel Bowditch. This act separated him even further from the crew. And his loneliness increased.

One evening, oblivious to the chilling breeze, Nat leaned on the leeward rail half watching the shadow patterns shift as the light breeze played fitfully across the waves. Lost in his own mood, he was unaware for some time that another soul had joined him. It was Buck, the Kanaka, a barrel-shaped man, about as tall as Nat, but more than fifty pounds heavier.

His bare arms were the most muscular Nat had ever seen, and his round brown face — after his frightening first impression — the friendliest.

"Hello, Kamanga," said Nat, giving the native his formal

name and trying to swallow the lump of homesickness in his throat.

"Buck," the man slapped himself on the chest. "Kamanga is shore name. Buck is longtime boat-steerer. We be friends. Buck friends with ever'body. You like this ship too. Men good. Cook good." He peered into Nat's face like a child looking at a stranger. "You sad little while, then no sad. Leave home here? Nice homes all over world. You see."

"You're certainly a long way from home," said Nat, making conversation.

"Not too much," Buck replied. "Many years the *Mingo* is home. Mr. Goodwin got captain to sign me on from my home place. He helped me be good seaman an' be good man too. Before him Buck jus' hungry native boy. Much better this way."

"Were you with my father long?"

"Days . . . days . . . days. Many, many days. He very good man. Like father for me too." He looked at Nat. "You don't mind we be brothers?"

"I don't mind," said Nat.

Thoughts of his father flooded his mind. "Buck. Will Captain Bradner . . ."

Buck held up a huge hand. "Captain is sick in his head I think sometimes. Sometimes he's nice. Sometimes he's terrible. He's good to Buck. You stay away from him."

A group of men came on deck for their evening smoke before turning in, and Buck drifted away to join them.

He left Nat a bit cheered up. "At least someone aboard likes it," he told himself. "It can't be all bad."

By the third day out, Nat had picked up most of the simpler facts of life aboard by watching how the others did things and by asking questions. The second mate, Joe Picard, was a naturally mean man, but Mr. Flanders and Providence Santos, the third mate, helped him when either saw that Nat really wanted to learn. But no one offered him companionship, and Tub Gibbons, who slept in the bunk below, seemed actively to dislike him.

With easygoing friendliness Nat had tried to get along with him. Once when Tub was working on a half-finished piece of intricate scrimshaw — an enormous tooth he was fashioning into a cribbage board — they came close to friendliness.

"Is that a whale's tooth?" Nat asked.

"Yup," said Tub.

"What'll it be when you're finished?"

"A whale's tooth," said Tub, and he roared with laughter. "I ain't makin' it," he explained. "The whale did that. Get it?"

"I get it," Nat grinned. "But what's the whale makin' out of it now?"

Tub took a minute to figure that one out. Then he grinned too. "Shucks, I ain't as big as a whale. . . . I'm pretty good size though ain't I? . . . and real tough too. This is a cribbage board — used to be a sperm whale's tooth. Biggest I've seen in ten years a-whalin'." He held it out for Nat to see.

"Ten years! Have you been to sea that long?"

"Started when I was fifteen. Ain't never left off. Prob'ly the best seaman there is."

"Don't you ever want to be a boat-steerer or have your own ship?"

"If they want to give it to me who deserves it, all right.

But you don't catch me workin' extra for it. I give 'em fair work for fair wages an' that's that." He scowled.

Hoping to change the subject, Nat quickly said, "You certainly know how to carve that bone."

"But don't let that fool you!" Tub continued truculently. "I'm a sight better seaman than some of them with harpoons to heave . . . an' a double sight better than any as come aboard fresh . . . an' I mean *any*." He glowered at Nat, but Nat put him off politely.

"You're certainly a better seaman than I am, Tub, if that's what you mean. Some day I hope I can do things as well as you do."

"Prob'ly you never will," Tub admitted. "An' in the meantime don't forget I'm cock-o'-the-walk around here."

He went back to his scrimshawing and Nat climbed topsides for a breath of fresh air.

On the fourth day the weather turned wet, and the crew was constantly forced together in the damp forecastle.

Nat lay in his bunk reading by the dim light of the swinging lantern. To get full advantage of what light there was, he had to lean partly over the edge of his cubby, as though listening avidly to the chatter of the crew. The bunks clung along the sides of the ship, making an ill-shaped communal area of less than ten feet square which had to serve as bedroom, living room, and dining room for sixteen men.

Mostly the men lay in their bunks or sat bent over on them facing toward the center of the space. The stale air was thick with the smells of tar and tobacco, wet clothing and sweat.

With the changing of the watch, Tub Gibbons

clumped heavily into the quarters. He stripped his wet clothes from his barrel body and tossed them in a heap on the deck. Reaching into his sea chest, he pulled out a dry shirt and slipped it over his heavy shoulders. As he pulled it down, he saw Nat hanging over the edge of his bunk.

"Reading," he growled. "You sure use up more than your share of light!" Nat saw that the man was in a bad temper. Blaming it on a nasty watch, he kept his peace.

"What d'ye ever expect to get by that?" Tub continued. "Hey, answer when I speak to you!"

Nat looked up from his book. "This book is on navigation by a man named Bowditch. I expect to learn to navigate."

Tub turned to the crew, a willing audience for anything which would break the monotony of their lives. "Wants to learn navigation, an' he don't know a royal truck from a main brace." The men who had been lying back came up on one elbow to see the fun.

"A man has to learn," Nat remarked.

"Why don't ye ask the captain?" one of them cracked in a falsetto. "You're too good for the forecastle anyhow."

"Look," said Nat, tossing his book back into the bunk. "I ask questions, but I don't ask favors. And I certainly don't get any given to me."

Gibbons taunted Nat again: "Mr. Flanders," he tried to mimic Goodwin's flat, husky tones. "How d'ye step a new mast? Mr. Flanders, why is the harpooner called the boat-steerer, sir? Mr. Flanders, do you have a stah chaht, sir, please, sir? Go live with 'em if you love 'em so much."

At that remark, Nat swung his feet over the side of the bunk.

"Back in the rack, sonny," another crew member called out. "You're getting out of your class with Tub."

Nat had no fear of Tub, or any other man aboard. He wasn't much of a whaleman, he knew, but he could fight with the best of them, and take his licking if he had to. He measured Tub for size and decided that, big as the older man was, he'd not be too much to take.

"Gonna show me what's what, hey, laddie?" Tub crooned, one arm against the overhead. "Don't try it, laddie, don't try it."

Nat hesitated, thinking, not of the fight, but of the aftereffects. Three days out and mixed up in a forecastle brawl over nothing. A brawl now, win or lose, would do him no good.

"That's better, laddie, back to your 'ittle book." Tub pressed his argument. He intended to stay top dog in the crew's quarters.

The call for mess rang out.

"My turn to fetch it," Nat said calmly and swung to the deck. He stood two inches taller than Gibbons and his shoulders were just as broad. He started to brush past on his way to the ladder.

"Don't push me, Goodwin," breathed Tub right into his face. Nat looked calmly down into the angry eyes and kept right on going.

"No fight now, Tub," pleaded Limey Bartlett. "We'll miss our dinner."

As Nat started up the ladder, he heard Eph Blackstone's slow drawl, "Ye called him that time, Tub, but can ye keep him down?"

They doled the meat from the common bucket in the time-honored way of whalers. Limey Bartlett sat blind-folded, back to Nat. Then Nat speared a piece of meat on the end of his knife. "Who gets it?" he asked. The blind-folded man called out a name until each member of the crew had his hunk of boiled beef. Every man had an equal chance for the choice bits.

Men's emotions ebb and flow. After mess, when Nat climbed back into his bunk and picked up his book, no one paid any attention, least of all Tub Gibbons in the bunk below.

Tub remained bully of the forecastle although there was tension in the air whenever Nat and he were below to-gether. Nat avoided trouble, however, and even in a ten by ten cockpit, it takes two to make a quarrel.

Once when Tub backhanded little Limey Bartlett for sitting on Tub's sea chest, Nat almost rose up. But it was not until a warm, moonlight night when they were on a long reach that the blowup came.

Most of the crew was on deck enjoying the balmy air, listening to Tony Freitas play his guitar. Nat idly watched the moon path glittering black and gold on the sea.

There was a sharp smack. Pete DuBois, the cabin boy, stumbled across Nat and fell on the deck. Before the prostrate boy could rise, Tub was standing over him. He kicked him heavily in the ribs and hauled back his foot for the next swing. Nat reached out and grabbed his ankle.

"Don't kick the kid, Tub," he said quietly. "He's not your size." He relaxed his grip.

"Mind your own business," growled Tub and again dug his toe into the boy's ribs.

Nat got to his feet. "You heard me. Kickin' a kid's no man's business."

"Shut up, or you'll get it yourself." Tub was ugly to-night.

"You'll never kick me, Gibbons. I'm too near your own size, and you know it." The men lying on deck jumped to their feet and clustered along the rails.

Before the last one made it, Gibbons rushed at Nat, head down. Nat was ready for him. He didn't try to side-step. As Gibbons' doubled-up form reached him, Nat raised his knee and at the same time brought both hands down hard on the back of Gibbons' head. Tub went to his knees but was up in an instant and back for more. Bullies may may or may not be cowards at heart. Tub was no coward. He was a brawler, and he loved to fight. He fought with wild swings and animal-like rushes, hoping to catch his opponent with flailing fist or to butt him to the deck with his great weight. Goodwin, taller and faster on his feet, had plenty of strength for this encounter. He planned his fight and took advantage of every wild swing to get in a solid counterpunch. Suddenly, as Tub came in with an-other rush, Nat turned and flipped the heavy man up on his hip and over his shoulder. Tub hit the deck flat on his back and lay gasping. Nat let him lie.

In a few seconds Gibbons rose to a crouch. The moon-light glinted on a blade in his hand.

Before Nat was fully aware of the change the fight had taken, his right forearm was dripping blood. He caught Tub's arm with his own left hand, twisted hard and rushed Gibbons backward toward the rail. As the big man's back thudded into the timber, the knife slipped from his loos-ened grip and fell with a faint splash into the sea.

Barely conscious, Tub had no fight left in him. Nat left him lying in the scuppers and quickly wrapped his own shirt around his forearm. The whole fight had lasted only three or four minutes, but it saw the downfall of a dictator.

By the time Captain Bradner reached the foredeck, the action was over.

"You all know there's to be no fighting aboard a ship of mine. Who was it?" His crisp tone meant business.

"I, sir." Nat was still breathing heavily, squeezing his forearm tight to stop the rush of blood.

"You, Goodwin, and Gibbons, of course. I expected it of Gibbons, but it's a black mark against you, Goodwin. It goes in the log as common brawling, and a five-dollar fine. Unless you've got a good . . . excuse. Have you?"

"No, sir." Nat squeezed tighter on his arm, but already he felt the wetness through his shirt. Captain Bradner saw the stain, black in the moonlight, spreading through his shirt.

"Who had the knife? Gibbons?" No one spoke. Gibbons struggled to his feet and then sagged against the rail. He said nothing.

"I must have cut my arm on the rain barrel, Captain." It was some relief to know that he didn't have to conceal the wound, and he raised his hand up to his shoulder to reduce the flow of blood.

"One of you had a knife." The captain's cold tone rang in Nat's buzzing head. "I want you to tell me whose knife it was."

"Captain," said Nat. "There's no knife on deck. You can search me or search Gibbons. Ask the other men if there's any knife on deck. There's no need for criminal charges."

"Let's see your arm," the captain abruptly changed the subject. "Will it stop you working?"

"No," said Nat, hoping he wouldn't faint. "It won't."

"Have Mr. Flanders bandage it at once." The captain dropped his hand. "And one of you lies. Live with that on your manly chests, my brave boys. I'll trust neither of you till one of you tells me." He went directly to his cabin.

The arm hurt Nat for a few days, but the wound began to heal rapidly in the sea air. He favored it a bit on his long climb to the lookout, holding more tightly than ever to the shrouds with his left hand. Without being asked and never mentioning it, Sal Thurston simply did more than his share until Nat was able again.

Even when working beside him on the horses, Gibbons didn't speak. The rest of the crew, however, had changed. At last he was accepted by them, and the tenseness that had existed for so long in the forecastle was dispelled.

There was a change in the officers' attitude toward him, too, however, and he was worried by it.

His interest in the ship and in navigation had continued to increase. Lately he had begun to think that his career, like his father's, might be in whaling. To rise in it he had to be thought well of by the men above him. And now none of the officers would believe either Gibbons or Goodwin until the guilt was made clear. Both were possible liars and brawlers.

Nat had no idea how to clear himself of his undeserved reputation, yet he knew instinctively that these seamen had little sympathy with apologizers, second-guessers, whiners, sea-lawyers, and feather merchants. And simply by holding his tongue he took the first step toward building respect.

Chapter 4

ONE MORNING as Nat came up on deck he immediately sensed a change. The watch was more alert, the men moved more briskly and shouted cheerily back and forth as they worked. Captain Bradner, standing near the helmsman, pointed toward the horizon. The helmsman, Tony Freitas, smiled, nodded, and altered course a couple of points to port.

In the direction Captain Bradner indicated, Nat saw a low-lying bank of light gray clouds clustered on the horizon. As his gaze focused he thought he saw the top of a mountain sticking up through one, then another farther off. When the captain had gone below to breakfast, Nat walked back to the helm to ask Tony about their new course.

"It's land," said Tony, quivering with excitement. "Cape Verde. We go into Perequica Bay. It's my home, São Nicolao. That big mountain's Monte Gorde . . . not the flat top, that's what-you-call-it — Sugar Loaf. But the tall one . . . at the feets beginning of it is our house."

"When were you there last?" asked Nat.

"Three, four years . . . I left. Shipped out on *Manhasset*. Dismantled round Cape Horn. Shipped on *Mingo* out of Chile — Valparaiso. . . . My wife . . . mother . . . father . . . *right there*." He grinned again and pointed with his beardless chin. "Tomorra, I'll see 'em. Oh, boy."

As he talked he almost unconsciously gave a spoke on the big mahogany wheel or took back a couple, constantly keeping a bit of weather helm in the rather light southwest breeze.

Although Nat didn't begrudge Tony his visit home, the thought made him homesick again, and he strolled forward to the foredeck. He saw Manuel leaning against the starboard rail moodily watching the land approach through its clouds. Manuel was the only person within thousands of miles who knew what "home" meant to Nat. Nat naturally gravitated toward him in his loneliness.

Both in time and distance Nat was far from home — so far that he was tugged in two directions, like a compass needle trying to point both north and south at the same time. He was as firmly determined as ever to find the atoll which was his father's prison, but now he realized with some remorse the lonely, hard life he had left his mother to live. He wished that he had been a bit kinder when he said good-bye. And he hoped that she had not misunderstood his eagerness to go as lack of love for her and the home she had made them. He resolved to write her a letter — a long letter — soon.

"You see that Tony? He's got the job you gotta have."

Manuel greeted him brusquely, shattering Nat's thoughts of home.

"What do you mean?"

"He's in the captain's boat. Bow oar. You gonna get ashore to find your father on any islands you better get in that boat. Captain always goes ashore."

"And just how do I go about getting into the captain's crew?"

"I'm dumb," said Manuel, spitting tobacco juice over the side. "You're smart. Everybody knows that too. You figure it out."

They dropped anchor in Perequica Bay, and the word was passed to ready the captain's boat.

In the forecastle Tony dug out the clean clothes he had been saving so long for just this occasion, greased and brushed his hair until it looked enameled — and shaved.

As the boat crew threw off the fall, Captain Bradner hollered up to Mr. Flanders. "I'm going to call at the Customs House, then pick up some pumpkins and sweet potatoes. I should be back in about three hours." The mate waved acknowledgment and the boat shoved off.

Sooner than anyone expected it to return, the captain's boat came alongside. There was one empty thwart and the missing man was Tony Freitas. Without a word to anyone, Captain Bradner went directly to his cabin. Before the boat was hoisted and the fresh provisions lugged off to the galley, however, the whole crew had the word.

Almost before the captain had entered the Customs House to share a glass of Madeira with the customs' officer, Tony had taken off. In his excitement, he simply jumped and ran.

The customs' officer was home in bed with a touch of

island fever, so Captain Bradner went directly to the market place. Shortly, a couple of donkeys led by a dark-skinned, hollow-cheeked Cape Verdean brought four great baskets full of vegetables to the whale boat.

"Where's Freitas?" demanded the captain.

"He took off," said Gibbons slowly. "This is where he lives."

"He belongs to the ship," snapped the captain. "He signed his papers in New Bedford. Until this cruise is over, he's mine."

"He'll be back, Captain," put in Joe Governo nervously. "He didn't jump ship. Didn't take clothes or nothin'! We didn't expect you for two, three hours."

"He was to stand by. He isn't here, so he jumped ship. Take me back aboard."

Deprived of his drink, missing the chance to talk with someone he wanted to see, "deserted" by one of his own crew, the captain had worked himself into a tight-lipped rage. And the men knew what that could mean. Silently they bent to the oars.

Nat had the morning watch. Just before dawn a light skiff rowed by an old man came up to the ladder. Freitas rose to the stern, patted the bowed old shoulders, and nimbly scrambled aboard.

"Good to see you," Nat greeted him. "The captain was really upset by your going. . . . Did you have a good time?"

"I saw my people," said Tony. And he quietly eased through the hatch to the gloom of the forecastle.

At dawn the ship got under way. At eight o'clock the grim-faced captain assembled the men.

No one had to tell Nat that something was wrong. The

crew, without a sound, lined up, and the very air carried the smell of apprehension.

"Freitas." Captain Bradner turned to the third mate, Joe Picard. "Bring him forward."

Picard, his thin lips curling back over his yellow teeth in a horrid smile, motioned and Tony stepped forward.

"Jump ship, eh . . . jump my ship, eh."

"I came back," Tony said simply, "myself."

"So you did . . . so you did," said the captain looking down at him coldly. "So you're here, now, in front of me. I didn't have to hunt you down. But you jumped ship, my lad, and you're here for punishment." He wheeled toward the mate. "Twenty lashes," he snapped.

"Tied in the riggin'!" added Picard with relish.

"What harm did he do?" In his astonishment Nat's words came out in a shaking voice hardly his own.

Every eye turned to him, but only the captain spoke. "Harm? Harm?" he began mildly. "There is no harm done. Aboard a whaler we live surrounded by harm, lad, until 'harm' loses all meaning. Here there is only the ship — the ship is the world and all men on it must obey or there will be nothing but anarchy and destruction. And who must they obey?" His voice was rising in intensity and his shining eyes looked deep into Nat's. "Who must they obey? They must obey *me*. For I am the captain. And the captain is *God*. Do you understand, now, lad? The ship is the world and I am *God*."

"You are our captain," cut in the firm deep voice of Jim Ward, the third mate's boat-steerer, "and we will obey you. But you are not God."

The captain's fury passed. His eyes went almost blank and he whispered, "No, I am not God." He turned again to the third mate. "Twenty lashes," he said as though he were saying good morning and stepped to one side.

It was the first time Nat had ever seen man punish man, and it made him sick. He did not vomit, but the strength drained from his arms and a hard ball formed in his stomach. Gradually the sensation of weakness was replaced by rising anger at the whole world.

Strangely, his reaction to the punishment was exactly opposite to that intended. During the flogging he was drawn close to Freitas, the "wrong-doer," and felt disgust and dislike rise toward the "justness" of his leader. He sensed the equal sympathy of the men around him, and knew for the first time that "the crew" is more than a collection of individuals; it is a living unity with group thoughts, group emotions, and capable of group action — like mutiny — which the individuals themselves might never take.

When it was over, Freitas was nearly unconscious, his back like raw meat. The men made him a pallet in the shade by the windward rail where he might be more comfortable than in the heat below.

Big Buck carried him over and placed him face down on it. Manuel brought a bucket of water and gently bathed the suffering man. Frenchy, the cook, came with a dipper and said, "Here, drink this."

Tony shook his head, but Frenchy insisted. "It's water and a spoonful of vinegar. It stops some of the hurt."

Mr. Picard came hurrying over. "Vinegar, you say, Frenchy. Here, give it to me. I'll bathe his wounds." He laughed with the sound of joy. "There's nothin' like vinegar on an open cut to make a man sing. Give it here I say." And he started to take it away from the fat cook.

"You wouldn't," Nat said in amazement. And Picard turned toward him.

"I wouldn't, hey. And why not? The dirty rat got himself in this mess didn't he? We'll teach him what's right. Give it here I say."

Buck reached out his big paw toward Frenchy. "I give it to Tony to drink, Cookie." And he took the dipper away as he looked coolly into Picard's hard black eyes.

"I order you . . ." Picard began.

"Captain orders me, Picard. You 'member once before . . . I am Kamanga, captain's harpooner, not Picard's." Calmly, Buck sat down by the injured man. Tense with fury Picard pulled a belaying pin from the rail and started for the back of Buck's head with it.

"Mr. Picard." Manuel's voice was almost as soft as usual but some tone in it stopped the mate abruptly. Nat saw Manuel stroking the hair at the back of his neck with the haft of his knife. "You hurt Buck an' the captain would bury you for sure. I think he would curse you as you sank, but I know he would bury you." To Nat's surprise Picard returned the belaying pin to its proper place and simply walked away. "What'll he do now?" Nat asked.

"Nothin'," said Manuel, "until he gets a chance. He just likes to see people suffer, that's all."

As Buck held the dipper, Nat wiped the sweat from Tony's brow. "At least you saw your family," Nat said. "You have that to think about."

"I do," said Freitas, his liquid eyes still mirroring their physical pain. "My wife died las' mont', an' my little boy."

While they were furling the topgallant at sundown, Gibbons sidled along the horse until he was close to Nat. "You were lucky today, boy, an' don't forget it. The captain

ain't no man you can talk back to or fight like me. The captain's the captain. He can break your head, flog you, keelhaul you, even hang you, and not a man will lift a finger to help you out. That's just the way it is. The captain's the general, the president, and all the judges. Just stay out of his way." Then he added somberly, "An' the captain we got may be losin' his buttons."

Nat never again forgot that the captain, even by whim, could ruin all of his plans to rescue his father. He had learned that wariness must be one of his rules of survival.

He became more conscious than he had ever been before of the rights of individuals. He treated people with a growing courtesy instead of the shy brusqueness of a young farm boy. But at the same time he insisted that other people recognize his own rights.

The following morning about ten o'clock, big Buck was standing alone in the eyes of the ship. Suddenly he let out a shout. "Blackfish! Blackfish! Big school to starboard."

Captain Bradner was on deck. "Man the boats . . . lower away . . . first boat to sink a harpoon gets tobacco all around." His eyes roved across the deck as the men below tumbled out of the forecastle. He pointed to Nat. "You. Take Freitas' oar." And as simply as that, Nat had his place in the captain's boat.

Beside him Manuel grinned. "I knew you'd get in somehow. Keep plannin' now. You got the brains. An' the luck."

As the *Mingo* hove to, all four boats were put in the water. Blackfish were hardly big enough to be really valuable — occasionally one might yield thirty gallons of low-grade oil — but they could be chased and harpooned

so they serve to sharpen up the crew for the real hunting
to come.

Nat had handled an oar on deck, sitting in a whaleboat
pulling air under Mr. Flanders' direction. He was grati-
fied now to find that he could get onto his thwart and
handle his oar reasonably well.

Buck was the boat-steerer. He took his place in the bow,
one leg braced against the gunwale, his great harpoon a
toy in his brown paw, and held his position like a bird dog
on point. They pulled hard and they pulled long, but the
school was moving fast into the wind, and they couldn't
close it.

Nat found that pulling his oar was not so much of a
trick as he had feared. He was afraid that he might catch
a crab during a chase, but he didn't have to worry. He
liked the solid bite of the ash blade into the water and the
rhythm of the swing made the blood tingle to his toes.

At last the captain swung his steering oar, and they
started back toward the ship. Suddenly he swept the oar
hard to starboard.

"Pull!" he shouted. "Pull for your lives! Pull . . . pull
for the first one! We'll get him, Bucko, my boy. Pull! A
blackfish, men, 'tween us and the ship."

Following the swing set by Gibbons' broad sweating
back, the crew made the ash oars bend and spring as they
really leaned into them in earnest. The excitement of the
chase was in them, and Nat felt a harbinger of the great
thrill that hunting the world's largest animal would give
him later.

"Stand by your oars," barked the captain. Buck grunted
as he heaved his harpoon with force enough to cleave solid
oak. Beside Nat the line began to flick out of the keg. A

quick scramble and Captain Bradner was in the bow, lance
in hand. And Buck was in the stern, at last the "boat-
steerer."

A sixteen-foot blackfish with a harpoon in him can't put
up too much of a fight, and soon the captain gave it the
coup-de-grace.

"Ain't worth a damn," muttered the captain. "Not
enough fat on him to feed the fire." Contemptuously he
hacked out the harpoon point with his lance. He saw Nat
looking the fish over carefully and explained, "He's an old
one probably couldn't stay up with the pod when they
speeded up."

"How do you know that he won't give much oil?" Nat
asked, curiously.

"Can't really tell you. The way his carcass looks, how
the lance entered, how he feels on the line, how the harpoon sank in. It's somethin' of all those things. But I *know*
. . . and you will too before we get a dozen. You've got
the makin's of a whaleman . . . and you pull a good oar."

He returned to the stern sheets and again took over
the steering oar as they swung back for the ship.

The captain's words set the blood pounding in Nat's
tired body again, and he felt the glow that unexpected
praise can give. The discomforts and inconveniences at sea
were forgotten for the moment; Nat was sure he wanted
to be a whaleman. As they pulled steadily back toward
the *Mingo,* his heart gave another lift, for he knew that
now he was sure to keep a place in the captain's boat.
What would the next step be in his plan to rescue his
father?

Lost in daydreams, he was dimly aware of the captain's

voice saying, "Your oars." But the message didn't quite get through.

"Goodwin! Damn it! You clumsy farmer!" the captain bellowed. There was a splintering crash as Nat's big oar struck the side of the ship. The handle smacked him in the chest so hard it knocked him backward off his thwart. Then the tholepin let go, and the long oar trailed uselessly alongside.

The captain's tirade was short because he had the job of getting under the davits and hoisting the whaleboat aboard. But the net result to Nat was disastrous. Labeled a clumsy clod who handled an oar like a hoe, he was assigned the job of shipkeeper along with the fat cook, the crippled carpenter, and the cabin boy.

Chapter
5

For MANY DAYS the *Mingo* rolled tediously along on a general southwesterly course, making for the Cape. The trade winds were a sailor's delight and they blew steadily without squalls or fitful changes of direction. The watches did little more than check the running rigging and swab down the decks with sea water.

During the day the copper sun burned down from a brazen sky, tanning the white New England skins until they almost matched their dark Cape Verdean shipmates.

Over half the men grew beards, then kept them hacked with scissors to about an inch or so. Because fresh water was something to be treasured, they seldom washed, but usually ran a comb or brush through hair and beard once a day. Those who shaved used straight razors honed sharp on a strap of leather and shaved without benefit of soap, though they did get hot water from the galley. They shaved on Sunday, and that lasted for a week.

Beards, and what to do with them, were on Nat's mind because his own upper lip was developing a few blond hairs and under his cheekbones the hair made irregular light-colored patches against his tanned skin. But what really bothered him was the hairs that grew right out of his chin. He tried to ignore them, but he couldn't. His fingers without any command from Nat, would sneak up and begin feeling for the long, thin scragglers. The only other person aboard who ever seemed to notice Nat's beard was Tub Gibbons, who looked at Nat one Saturday and said, "Either get used to it or cut it off!" Then he grinned. "Hey, I'll bet you ain't even got a razor!"

Nat blushed, and got angry because he blushed and because he didn't have a razor. But Tub, in a friendly mood, continued.

"Tomorrow I'll let you take mine, and I'll show you how to use it."

The following day, Nat sat on an empty keg, looked into a sliver of mirror nailed to the foremast, and had his shave while the crew stood around joking about his lack of technique. Even Mr. Flanders came forward to join the fun. It was a pleasant day, all things considered, and they had plum duff at dinner too.

At night the stars of the southern sky, led by the Southern Cross, hung luminous in black velvet, brighter and closer than Nat believed possible.

The remembrance of his blunder with the oar was still humiliating. And the fact that the captain had assigned him shipkeeper, instead of member of a boat crew, was a bitter pill indeed.

To a boy of fifteen, the excitement of whaling was all in the chase. The thought of leaning on a rail waiting while the others shoved off in the boats was enough to make any lad wonder why he'd left home for life on a sooty, stinking ship. To Nat, particularly, being assigned ship-keeper meant that getting ashore in search of his father would be complicated almost to the point of assured failure. He saw no solution.

He kept plugging away at his daily tasks, always trying to do them a little better, a little faster than he had the day before. And he kept at the Bowditch he had borrowed. He and Mr. Flanders hit it off well. The excitable mate was drawn to the quiet boy who didn't ever seem to lose his calm. When Nat missed a point in navigation, Mr. Flanders' exasperation would mount higher and higher until he was pounding one muscular fist into the other as though he could drive the point into Nat's head. Book learning comes slowly when you have to get it between the distractions of the ship and fighting the feeling of being different from the rest of the crew.

Unlike his friends, however, Nat was already looking ahead to the voyage after this one. And he didn't intend to stay the lowest-paid man on the ship. He was smart and had done well at school, but his persistence was even more important. Even though progress some days was painfully slow, and Mr. Flanders' stinging taunts rang in his memory for hours, each day a few more pages were behind them and a few less remained. The end of the book was in sight, and Nat had reasonable confidence in his ability to navigate.

The long run downhill toward Brazil in fine weather gave the officers a chance to get ahead on the ship's work.

With the old ship wallowing along at a steady six knots, Mr. Flanders started the crew checking every bit of running and standing rigging. He was a brash, headstrong fellow only about twenty years old. But though the crew thought him a bit of a wildcat in a whaleboat, they admitted he knew whaling and he knew ships.

"That Horn's always trouble," he told Nat. "When we round the Horn, we want everything right. The captain's a real stickler, a topnotch seaman — and one of the best at rounding the Horn." Then he added somberly, "Speaking of the captain, Goodwin, and we won't again, let me warn you that he does strange things at times — almost like a madman it seems. So watch your step and don't cross him."

Nat started to question him further but Mr. Flanders held up his hand. "No more. We're not discussing the captain. I just thought a warning to you only fair. Now back to work."

First they went up the ratlines a step at a time replacing every frayed crosspiece, then onto the horses where the men stood when furling the sails. The stays were in top shape because the owners had just replaced a mast, and the fitters in the shipyard had checked them then. Halyards looked frayed and whiskery to Nat, but Mr. Flanders assured him that they were sound. The tension and the weather lifted a whisker or two, he explained, but there were no points where the fibers had begun to break. The braces, used to set the spars at the proper fore and aft angles, and the sheets, which controlled the setting of the sails, were checked last. Then Mr. Flanders turned his attention to the sails.

Each in its turn was spread out in the tropic sun on

the broad foredeck. The crew went over them minutely, and "Sails" followed with his palm and needle to pick up where stitches had rotted away and to sew on regular patches where the canvas had torn.

Three triangular sails footed to the great jib boom: the flying jib, the jib, and a fore-topmast staysail.

On the foremast, the *Mingo* carried four square sails — nearest to deck a foresail or "forecourse," above it a fore-topsail, then a fore-topgallant, and next to the clouds a foreroyal. On the mainmast the same sails — mainsail, maintop, main-topgallant, and main royal. And on the much smaller mast aft, a spanker and a gaff topsail, both set fore and aft, like small boat sails.

Anxious to get onto the grounds and start making money, Captain Bradner elected not to stop on the east coast but to round the Horn, then put in far up the west coast, in Peru, for fresh supplies and water.

As the *Mingo* approached Cape Horn the very character of the sea below and the sky above underwent an ominous change. Gone were the steady trades, and the men began to earn their keep tempering the canvas to the fitful gusts and contrary squalls. The blue sky turned leaden as they crossed 50 degrees south latitude, and the sun and the stars appeared only at rare intervals between scudding clouds.

The sea, too, lost its color and became a darker gray even than the brooding sky. The surface took on an oily look and long strips of black water were streaked and wiped away by the rising wind. Against the tropical blue, whitecaps had made a pretty touch, but now they seemed like the teeth of impatient wolves snapping and snarling at the passing hull.

There was less roll to the ship but much more pitch as she climbed the steep watery hills only to bury her nose when she slid down on the other side.

The spars creaked and the rigging sang before the increasing wind. The gentle sway to and fro, that Nat had come to expect, was gone and the crosstrees seemed to whip back at the end of each roll, settle for a minute at the center, then snap swiftly the other way only to whip back again.

Since his second day aboard, Nat had never been seasick, and this motion did not affect his stomach. But his old fear of height began to come back again, so it was with real relief that he reached the deck whenever his watch was over.

Into the fourth night the wind continued to rise, the strong westerly blowing the waves into luminous whitecaps. By dawn the ship was surrounded by heavy seas, taking them well as a whaler should and holding to course under lightened canvas. No lookout was posted now, for until the weather broke there was little likelihood of spotting a whale and no possibility of lowering a boat.

The *Mingo* beat on almost into the teeth of the wind, now stripped to jib, topsails, and spanker. In the forecastle the men stayed warm enough, but the bantering stopped. The high-pitched shriek of the wind was with them always, and the dampness which storm brings had penetrated everything.

One noon as the crew was dividing up mess in the forecastle, the sea suddenly began to thunder against the hull, almost halting the ship with every shock.

"This is it," said Content Perkins to Nat. "Them's comin'

from the Pacific. Now you'll learn a thing or two boy. This is the Horn!"

Nat went on deck at once, partly to see what was going on and partly because being locked up in a drum was not to his liking. The gray waves had a greasy surface, and the yellow foam seemed not born of the water at all. Long streamers of ribbon weed made scars of black calm. But there was no great change in sea or sky. The waves were bigger and the wind stronger, veering into the northwest. They'd still have it in their teeth, thought Nat, at least for the next watch.

Buck was standing beside his whaleboat doing something to his great harpoon. Captain Bradner had the deck and Manuel was with him. Together they came forward across the slippery wet planking. The captain was pointing high in the rigging. Manuel nodded, took a coil of line, and started aloft. Nat looked up and saw the royal backstay, broken, whipping in the wind.

Manuel would have to climb almost to the truck before he could catch the end and make fast his new line. Involuntarily, Nat shuddered as he thought of that climb with the wind screaming in a man's ears and the sea shaking the ship like a boy shaking a small pear tree. Unless the backstay was replaced, however, there was a chance of losing the fore-topmast itself.

Manuel scrambled quickly up the ratlines, past the top, clung to his swaying ladder as the ship rolled to his side, then scrambled higher as the opposite roll began.

Nat watched the man with admiration. He certainly had the feel of a ship's rigging. Manuel reached the royal crosstrees and put one hand out for the swinging stay. Then it happened.

Manuel's head swung in a quick arc. The next instant he was dangling head down, one foot apparently caught in the shrouds.

Nat waited for Manuel to reach out and pull himself upright, but the limp body merely swung back and forth in empty space. Manuel was out cold. Any roll of the ship might dislodge his foot and send him hurtling into the sea, or smash him to the deck almost a hundred feet below.

Nat sprang into the rigging and raced for the top. A roll caught him before he was ready, and his feet slipped from the ratline. He clung grimly, praying that he would not lose his grip on the shrouds. As the ship started back the other way, his body pressed flat against the lines. His bare feet found the ropes, and he started upward again. Above him his friend's unconscious body still swung grotesquely upside down.

Edging out around the shrouds at the lower crosstrees, Nat almost lost his grip. His fingers were stiff from the strain and from fear. He was winded from the quick climb in the gale. He wondered how he could get Manuel down if he did reach him. But as he climbed the last ten feet his plan was made.

Pausing long enough to cut a piece of marlin from the ratlines, he tied Manuel's wrists together, then lashed them to a shroud. Nat quickly freed the foot caught above him and, holding Manuel's clothing with his free hand, carefully swung the body down toward the creaking yard. At last he slipped the tied wrists over his head and started to descend.

It took more strength than he had anticipated, and the strain made his already stiff hands numb. He prayed that the ratlines would hold their combined weight. And when the ship rolled toward them, he had to slip his arms around the ropes, for his hands were no longer of much use. Watching anxiously from the deck, Buck and Captain Bradner decided that Nat had the situation well in hand. Then just below the main span, when even Nat thought the worst was over, Manuel regained consciousness enough to realize their danger.

"Cut me loose, Nat," he mumbled. "I can make it from here." Reluctantly, but feeling that he might not make it with the two of them, Nat maneuvered Manuel's feet on to one ratline, his hands on to another, and worked himself out from under. He fenced Manuel against the ratline with his own body, drew his sheath knife and sliced the lashing between the wrists.

"I'm a'right," said Manuel, shakily taking a step down. Two slow steps later the ship lurched toward them again. Still only half-conscious, Manuel lost his grip and pitched backward over Nat's head into the empty air above the sea. Nat grabbed the Portuguese's clothing, but his fingers had no strength, and seconds later his semiconscious friend hit the cold waters below with a splash.

"Overboard — man overboard!" Nat yelled to the men below. Then he jumped into the icy sea to try to keep Manuel afloat.

The ship, buffeted by head winds and high waves, was making scarcely any headway so a few strokes brought Nat to the now-conscious Manuel.

"Lower de boat, Captain," said Buck springing up on the rail. But Captain Bradner shook his head.

"Not in this sea, Buck. There's not a chance."

Instantly Buck jumped into the whaleboat himself, gave

a quick glance to be sure the tubline was free, and poised himself in the stern sheets with his harpoon aimed directly at Nat.

The stick cleared Nat's head by less than a foot and bobbed up in the water behind him. Right across his shoulder lay the line.

"Tie 'im!" shouted Buck, but the advice wasn't needed. Manual and Nat had the line looped about their bodies and were ready for the strain.

The great sails began to flutter as Captain Bradner took a chance and headed the vessel into the wind. Fortunately the distance wasn't great, but both Nat and Manuel were blue and chattering when they were finally hauled aboard.

"Get 'im coffee, Cookie!" yelled Peckham from the wheel as he swung the heaving *Mingo* back on course.

"I have a little rum," said Captain Bradner. "Bring them to my cabin to get warm."

Buck shook the kinks out of the tubline and replaced his harpoon. Then he too went into the captain's cabin. Solemnly he placed his hand on Nat's shoulder. "You one brave man, boy," he said. "You an' Buck friends forever."

"A brave man, Goodwin," echoed Captain Bradner. "But a fool. By rights you'd still be out there, drowned."

Nat shivered harder as he took the first gulp of rum and hot water he had ever tasted. He didn't like it, but it certainly warmed him up.

Chapter
6

ONCE ROUND the Horn the ship soon gained the Peru current and a steady additional push north up the coast of Chile. The weather stayed cold and foggy, and the air was so damp that Nat could almost squeeze water droplets out of it with his bare fist.

They hugged the coast fairly tight, staying well to the east of 80 degrees E. longitude. Crosstree lookouts were still not posted because of fog. One day at about 45 degrees S. latitude, however, Joe Governo gave a shout from the bow. They had blundered across a lone bull sperm whale.

"Captain, may I take Goodwin along for the experience?" asked Mr. Flanders, one hand already on the gunwale of his whaleboat.

Captain Bradner didn't answer at once, which was unlike him. His eyes searched the mate's face as though looking for a challenge. Then his gaze shifted to Nat. Finally he made his slow decision. "All right. Take him in place of Bourne. But he belongs in my whaleboat when we're on the Grounds. Don't forget it." He turned toward Nat again. "An' don't learn any bad habits."

Nat started to reply but thought better of it. He liked Mr. Flanders, and feeling loyalty toward his friends was part of his nature. He took Bourne's place on the forward thwart and made his oar ready.

Mr. Flanders shouted, "Lower away."

The seas were heavy, but the old *Mingo* ploughed along at a good clip. With great skill, which he had, and equal luck, which he might not have, Mr. Flanders could pick a wave, drop his stern into the water slightly before the bow got wet and be off. If he misjudged, or luck ran against him, he could lose the fully equipped whaleboat and perhaps the men in it.

Captain Bradner shook his head disapprovingly. "Hold fast," he snapped to the men on the lines. "We'll make a lee." He headed the *Mingo* into the wind to slow her down. "We'll follow you with the ship, Mr. Flanders. If he changes course radically, let 'im go. This fog won't lift today, and it ain't worth losing an outfitted boat and her whole crew for five and forty barrels."

Mr. Flanders nodded, tight lipped in his contempt for all this caution. The men rowed hard, and Flanders whipped them on with his tongue. At first Nat felt exhilarated by the exercise, but soon his hands began to feel raw from the unfamiliar grip on the oar. Before long he broke into a sweat and began to breathe in deep gasps. Flanders kept driving them to greater and greater effort, but the whale, traveling fast, pulled away little by little and was soon swallowed up by the fog.

Making no attempt to hide his disappointment, Mr. Flanders flung the long steering oar to port and headed his crew at half speed toward the ship. Captain Bradner shouted and raved at them as a batch of no-good loafers, weaklings, runts, farmers, on and on until Nat began to believe that the captain really had lost his wits and might never stop. But at last he did, with the order that each day thereafter the crews would lower away and pull until they got into shape.

When he went below, Manuel came over to Nat. "You pulled a good oar. He'll put you in his boat again all right. He likes big ones in his own crew." His darting eyes saw the blisters on Nat's hands, and he nodded his head with satisfaction. "They're blistered in the right place. You're handling your oar right. Get some salt water and dip your hands in it now. It'll sting, but it'll toughen up your skin faster."

Not sure whether this was superstition or truth, Nat nevertheless did as he was told. The boats were lowered and pulled every day; his hands hurt for three or four days then calloused up into sturdy rowing tools.

Ten degrees farther north the captain abruptly changed course and ran due east for the coast of Chile. By now the weather had become balmy again. Skies were blue with scudding white clouds and the crew was back on regular watch schedule with lookouts manning the crosstrees.

Late one afternoon the lookout spied the sun hitting the snowcapped tops of the Cordilleras. Soon the captain identified Concepción and set his course into Talcahuano.

As they sailed into the harbor, just after sunrise, a heavily rigged, trim black sloop was weighing anchor. There was a brisk, efficient look about her and she flew the Stars and Stripes.

"It's the first time I ever heard of a Navy ship in the Pacific," Mr. Flanders said.

"An expedition was poking about a couple of years back," the captain replied. "I heard something about a fellow named Wilkes heading it, but that was just scientific research. This looks like business."

"It won't bother us none," Mr. Flanders said philosophically.

"Bother us none!" snorted the captain lowering the glass. "They'll be tellin' us where we can hunt an' where we can't . . . when we can go and when we can come . . . an' our crews will all get out of control knowing they can run like crybabies to the government if a captain or mate so much as don't say 'please' when he gives an order. You mark my words, Mr. Flanders, it's the end of decent whalin' if the government tries to keep order."

Mr. Flanders had his own thoughts on the subject, but there seemed to be no reason to keep the captain's fuse burning, so he wisely changed the subject.

"Last time I was in Chile," he said, "they'd just shot the president, Portales. Everybody seemed to like him, but he got shot anyhow. Wonder who's running things now?"

"I don't know," replied Bradner. "But I'll bet it's 'General' somebody or other. Talcahuano's good pickin's, too, and I'll bet the Commandante runs things his ways. Let's hope he likes Yankee whalers."

"Perhaps the Navy sloop was just paying the country's respects to him," Flanders suggested.

"That just might be it." Captain Bradner pulled his

ear lobe thoughtfully. "I'd like to be sure. I think I'll pay our respects to El Commandante too."

But his first meeting with El Commandante was not entirely social.

Penned up since they had left the Azores, the men secured ship in short order and piled into the whaleboats to stretch their legs ashore. To Nat's astonishment, both Manuel and Buck elected to stay aboard ship. Manuel wouldn't tell him why, but he learned later that on an earlier trip to Talcahuano little Manuel, caught in a barroom brawl, had saved himself and a beaten-up friend by throwing two knives. They escaped to their ship, but Manuel lived in fear of facing a double murder charge in this strange and violent port.

Buck's reason for staying aboard was simpler. "Everybody gets drunk. Buck don't. Makes me sick."

Nat went ashore with Joe Governo, Tony Freitas, and Ben Bourne, a first voyage man from Massachusetts who pulled bow oar in the second mate's boat. Aboard ship Nat saw little of Ben because they were in opposite watches and on different details. He knew the second mate better. Providence Santos was a quiet, soft spoken Cape Verde Islander who paid strict atttention to the business of whaling. As they hit the beach, he told them that the boat would return to the ship at midnight.

Talcahuano was an experience Nat never forgot. Because he was so young when he left home, his mother had exacted his promise not to drink until he was grown, and he intended to keep his word. Before the night was over, he was sure that he was the only man in the world not roaring drunk.

The town consisted of one dusty, dirty main street. The

building nearest the landing was a saloon, as were most of the other buildings on the *Camino Grande*.

The crowd in town — a mixed group of Spanish, *mestizos,* an occasional haughty Araucanian, and men from the six whalers swinging around their hooks in the harbor — was not really large, but it seemed to drift from one spot to another in a cluster of humanity. As a result, one saloon after another was jumping with excitement, then deserted.

Nat enjoyed the guitar playing and the native dances, which were certainly unlike anything he had ever imagined in Rhode Island. By eleven-thirty, however, he and Santos were ready to return and found their way to the shore.

There he learned that Ben Bourne and Tony had decided to jump ship and had sought out the Commandante to ask his help. Early in the morning, Captain Bradner received word of this.

After waiting until noon for the deserters, Captain Bradner ordered the waist boat lowered and told Nat he would pull an oar. They beached, leaving Dan Brink to guard the boat while Joe, Tub, and Nat fell in behind the captain.

The road, hot and dusty in the noonday sun, followed the curve of the beach for a short distance then turned toward the town square perhaps two hundred yards inland. The first building they passed was a saloon. Glassless holes in the adobe walls served for windows and a doorless entrance opened into the black depths beyond. The smell of stale *cerveza* hung heavy in the air. Smelly saloons just like it stood in seedy disarray along both sides of the narrow main street as the little band of Americans trudged along.

When they approached the square, a flat rectangle of dust with a single great spreading tree in the middle of it, Nat saw that a crowd was gathered there. The hum of voices and the high-pitched yapping of a dog made him uneasy. He glanced at big Tub, who seemed unconcerned about the whole thing, but Nat suddenly noticed that Tub was carrying a belaying pin and his seaman's knife was stuck loosely in his belt. As they entered the square, Nat could tell that the people were waiting for something to happen. Then he looked at the tree, the center of attention, and the sight struck him like a club.

Strung from a great limb by their thumbs, Ben and Tony teetered on the tips of their bare toes still trying to keep their joints from pulling asunder. Their bare backs, glistening with sweat, drew swarms of hungry flies. No one made any move toward them — either to hurt or to help. The people of Talcahuano simply watched.

Sitting alone on the shady veranda of the palace, his feet on the rail and a cool drink at his elbow, was El Commandante. Four or five soldiers in red-and-black uniforms were lolling on the steps, their guns stacked in a neat pyramid to one side.

With scarcely a glance at the suffering men, Captain Bradner and his men strode straight across the square toward the Commandante.

Without taking his heels off the rail the Spaniard waved toward a seat. Nat expected sparks to fly. Nothing happened. Captain Bradner sat down in the chair indicated and crossed leg over knee. Neither man spoke. When Nat glanced toward the horrible tree, he saw the look of desperate pleading on Ben Bourne's face.

"Captain," Nat said. "I'm going to cut them down."

Tiger fast, the captain towered above him. "Shut up," he snapped. "Those men are deserters — and they're mine. You make any move and you join them." His eyes were as glittering hard as they had been when poor Tony Freitas faced him off the Azores. Again Nat had the cold feeling that Captain Bradner was insane.

The muscles of the captain's jaw flexed and unflexed rhythmically as he clenched and unclenched the ragged teeth behind his parted lips. Abruptly he turned away and sat down.

Nat felt Tub's big paw on his arm. The thumb flipped toward the soldiers. Nat saw then that they had unstacked their guns and were standing — eyes on the Commandante. "It's up to the captain," Tub whispered. "He can buy them back . . . if he wants to."

If he wants to, Nat thought. What does Tub mean by that? But Tub said no more and merely shook his head, unwilling to talk when Nat turned toward him.

Finally, in excellent English, the Commandante spoke. "They are from your ship. Last night they talked about not going back aboard, Captain. They signed a paper which said so, Captain. I have it. But last night they committed a very grave crime, Captain. We do not want your criminal types. We have no jail. We must dispose of them — somewhere."

"They are my men," admitted Bradner. "They have signed my ship's papers for the duration of a cruise. Any other paper they sign, until that contract with me is complete, is not legal."

"So," smiled the Commandante. "Then you want the men."

Bradner looked impassively at the two pain-wracked

70

bodies. "I want the men. My crew must learn what it costs to jump ship on me. They will be punished, too, for the inconvenience they have caused in your happy town."

"How much?" asked the Commandante sloshing the ice in his rum-filled glass. "Talcahuano is a small port and the expenses incurred have been heavy."

"They are not much good as sailors. First cruise. I am teaching them the business."

And suddenly Nat realized that Captain Bradner was utterly without compassion. This whole talk was not to save Ben and Tony as soon as possible. It was to reduce the ransom price that would have to be paid.

"In dollars, U.S., one hundred each." The Commandante was playing poker now. His feet came off the rail. His body tensed as he swung his chair toward Bradner.

Bradner laughed shortly. "That's more than they earn on the whole cruise. They're not worth it."

"The price is firm at ninety dollars," purred the Commandante, "because our war is over and the mines once again in operation. For two able-bodied criminals, delivered, they pay me ninety dollars. I am giving you the first chance at that price because they are your countrymen."

"They are deserters," snapped the captain, "and deserters are nobody's countrymen. I will pay fifty dollars and no more."

The Commandante shook his head. "Eighty-five dollars it will have to be. Five off to save me the trouble of delivering them to the mines. My expenses, you know, were heavy in capturing these two." He waved toward the six uniformed soldiers, indicating that he had been forced to call out the army.

"I thought you said they came to you and signed a paper voluntarily."

"Yes," added the Commandante, "and the costs of paper and ink. Let us stop playing, Captain. The price is eighty-five dollars . . . each."

Once more Bradner glanced at the two men in the tree, and Nat thought the end of the bargaining had come at last.

It had. "Too much," said Bradner, rising. "Send 'em to the mines."

"Captain," blurted out Nat. "I'll pay it."

The captain looked at him coldly. "How? You don't even have credit, boy, on the ship. Future wages? Suppose you get killed before the future gets here? . . . And that is a possibility, you know."

Tub rose up beside Nat. "Stay out of it, Gibbons. You're not worth much yourself — and I'm being offered eighty-five dollars a head right here." The captain stared at the crew.

"Take one good look at that tree. And remember to tell your shipmates what happens to deserters."

He turned to the Commandante.

"I am sorry for the intrusion upon your time, Commandante . . . particularly when it follows so soon upon the intrusion by the Navy of my country." He watched carefully for any sign.

"*De nada,*" the Commandante replied graciously. "Your little Navy ship was merely provisioning for a long cruise on the whaling grounds. They are now over the horizon." He rose and bowed toward Captain Bradner. "If you change your mind, Captain, the men will be here until sundown."

"I will not change my mind, Commandante," Bradner replied.

"*Si*," nodded the Commandante. "*Buenos dias.*" And he walked inside.

Not a word was spoken while the men returned with Captain Bradner to the ship.

Chapter 7

THE INCIDENT at the square was still vivid in Nat's mind, as it would be for some time to come, and any thought of getting the captain to help him hunt for his father was almost dead. He knew that Bradner had no more sympathy for another man than Nat had for a fat chicken strutting in its yard.

Nat had never given much thought to the finer points of right and wrong. He had gone to church every Sunday back home; he knew what the minister had taught. He agreed with the "do unto others as you would have them do unto you," although he thought it pretty hard to follow. But he had never been convinced that to "turn the other cheek" was always right, and he lost interest entirely on the really fine points of theology.

Nevertheless he had a strong personal sense of how he felt a man should act, and by and large he tried to live up to it. He knew that his own code would have made him act differently toward the deserters. And because he was so sure that he was right, he felt a match for the captain. The surge of blood in his veins was powerful and exhilarating, but it brought with it recognition of his own responsibility as a leader. He resolved to talk to Manuel as soon as he could.

After the evening meal, Nat found Manuel up in the bow gazing longingly at the town he didn't dare set foot in. It was early for the revelry to begin, but already the plaintive notes of a picked guitar came softly across the water.

"Manuel," Nat began abruptly. "Now I know what happens to men who cross the captain. I don't want you to go on with our plan to save my father. There is too much risk for you."

Manuel, surprised by Nat's abruptness, misunderstood. "You don't want to try to save your father?" He looked at the boy searchingly, a bit puzzled.

"I can imagine what Captain Bradner would do to anyone he caught. It is not a chance you have to take. Why should you?"

"Because your father was a good man and he needs help. Do you think I am a coward who is afraid? There is danger from the captain, sure . . . there is danger from the natives much more. They might kill you, and then you would be dead. Dead men go to heaven. Is that bad?" He grinned his wry little grin and slapped Nat on the shoulder.

"You do not need to take the chance at all, Manuel," said Nat stubbornly.

Manuel shook his head. "You have been too much

around women. Sometimes, boy, a man must do good things because they are good things to do. If he dies, then he dies, but the good thing remains worth doing. Death can never be something to run away from, boy. Why you might stumble in running away and split your head on a rock!" He laughed at his own humor, and his relief at finishing his simple philosophy.

Nat shook his head. "I still can't ask you to take the risk for me."

Manuel's face grew hard and he grabbed Nat by the shirt front. "You are a good boy but don't get the big head. I took the chance in that bar in Valparaiso. I took the chance with that little statue aboard this ship for months. I took the chance to go get you and to bring Goodwin's son to this ship. I got you to help me. But don't get too big for your head. You ain't never fire a gun or throw a knife or even see a man killed. Alone you ain't nothing but . . ."

Intent on the heat of their own argument, both had forgotten where they were until a shadow fell across them and each felt a strong hand firmly grab his shoulder. Startled, they looked up into Buck's fierce scowling face.

"Not good," he said in his deepest voice. "Not good. You talk like this, captain he'll find out. You never even get close to Mr. Goodwin Island."

Nat felt Buck's grip relax as the giant leaned toward him and said quickly, "When the right time come, tell me. I talk native talk. I come 'longside you."

They heard Tub Gibbons' heavy tread on the ladder. Nat nodded quickly to the other two.

"I'll plan it in my head and tell you both when the time

comes." By the time Tub reached the deck the three were far apart.

The following day Manuel got a barrel end from Mr. Murchison, the cooper, and nailed it to the foremast four or five feet from the deck. He scratched a circle in the center of it to serve as bull's-eye and began to teach Nat how to throw a knife. It was surprisingly easy to do — within a week Nat was hitting the target steadily. To Manuel's great satisfaction, however, he could always find something which made *him* a little better with a knife. He could hit a little closer to the center, and he had the ability to throw from almost any position.

Nat had begun to watch Manuel and Buck more closely these days because he wanted to know the strengths and weaknesses of the men who might be with him on the island. Manuel, in particular, was a cause for concern. He had a queer nervous habit of coughing and clearing his throat. He wasn't strong. And he couldn't swim. But he had an almost fanatical belief that their mission would succeed — *he* was going to rescue the man who had befriended him. There was no question in his mind about that.

Buck was the perfect companion for scouting out the island. Strong, tough, a great swimmer, he spoke the native language and knew how natives thought and acted. He would be an invaluable ally. Yet he was friendly with Captain Bradner. . . . Nat decided he'd better find out more about Buck. He found him over by the waist boat honing the already razor-sharp lance. He came directly to the point.

"Buck," he said. "Why will you take a risk to try to rescue my father? What good will it do you?"

Buck looked at him gravely, thought a bit about the questions, then said, "My own people always fight the Kaneroans. They are very bad people. To fight them is good. To let them keep Mr. Goodwin is bad. Not to get him back is a weak man. I do not like inside me when I remember Mr. Goodwin. Captain Bradner is very wrong."

"But you seem very friendly with the captain, Buck. Couldn't you get him to rescue my father?"

Buck shook his head. "Many times I tried. But he never listens. He gets mad. . . . Captain Bradner has sickness in his head. It comes sometimes. My Tane — my god — says people sick in the head belong to him . . . need help so they will not do too much wrong. Tane tells us to help them."

"Would you jump ship?"

Buck shook his head. "Jump ship is wrong. But go get Mr. Goodwin is not jumping. Is big good. An' must do it, boy, then do it."

Doubts don't disappear completely with a reassuring word or two, but Nat went away feeling sure of Buck. His hatred of Kaneroans, his liking for Mr. Goodwin, and his realistic attitude toward the captain were clear. But could he be trusted to keep any secret?

The *Mingo* left Talcahuano at sunup of the third day. As the harbor grew smaller and smaller in the distance, Nat thought of Ben and Tony left behind either to die or to sweat out their lives in a hole in the ground. After the first day, no one in the crew ever mentioned the two men. Perhaps it was the enormity of punishment, or the thought that "it might have been me," or the guilty frustration of strong men who do nothing, or ancient superstition. Whatever the reason, Ben and Tony might never have been aboard the *Mingo* as far as her crew was concerned. The few who thought about the missing men kept their thoughts to themselves.

Captain Bradner set the course about one hundred miles off the coast in a gentle curve toward the Galapagos Islands, a month or so away. In the meantime they would watch for whales. The lookouts were halfhearted about their work, however, until they passed the twentieth parallel and turned north-northwest for the Archer Grounds. An occasional ship reported oil barrelled below that area, but any strike was considered lucky.

Any crew expected to work when they found whales on the grounds; aboard the *Mingo* the men honed their knives, washed their clothes, and prepared for a long period of sweaty, greasy, hard labor.

The cooper began digging bundles of staves out of the hold and knocked a barrel or two together just to get his hand in. Nat marveled at the tiny space the neatly nestled staves took compared to the vast amount of space the finished barrel enclosed. The staves were all precut; the cooper matched them up and hooped them with quick deft taps of his odd-shaped hammer.

The smith went over the harpoons, toggles, lances, and spades to be sure the weapons were ready for the chase. He checked the great iron cauldrons in the tryworks, each big enough to hold one hundred and thirty-six gallons of boiling oil, to be sure neither holes nor cracks would let the precious fluid leak away. He checked the blocks and tackle for the hundredth time to be sure the iron pins were not weakened by rust inside their wooden rollers, because soon hunks of blubber weighing a ton would be hoisted aboard.

The boat-steerers rechecked the three-foot wrought-iron harpoons and smoothed the five-foot-long hickory handles to perfection. They carefully laid down the three-stranded, tarred hemp lines, two hundred and twenty fathoms of it in each bucket, so that both ends were free. One end was hitched to the harpoon. The other had a loop spliced into it so that line from another boat could be attached to it if thirteen hundred feet was not enough.

The cook put an extra effort into his messes, thinking of the days in the near future when the crew would wolf down their food while they stayed right at the job.

But day followed empty day without a glimpse of a whale. During the first week, expectations were high. After that the crew muttered and grumbled that the captain was jinxed and might never get a whale, and finally the mates themselves grew short tempered and snapped out their orders as if they held personal grudges against everyone.

Fortunately Nat was, by nature and his mother's training, steady minded and gifted with common sense. He went through the trying period without complaining, maintaining that superstitious belief in a jinx was ignorance and nothing more. Because he was easy to work with, the mates began to give him more to do; because he did it well, he was given more authority and men worked well for him, young as he was.

But while the ship wallowed north, the crew moved their bedding to the decks to escape the stifling heat of the forecastle. Pushed nearly as much by the current as by the light fitful winds, the *Mingo* at last approached the equator, and word got around that they would go ashore for water at Isla Isabella.

"Remember." Manuel shook his thin brown forefinger at Nat. "This you must remember all about. It is your only dress rehearsal."

Nat nodded thinking that if his first act didn't go right he'd never get a second chance. "I'll watch everything," he promised gravely.

He felt Captain Bradner's eyes upon them. His thick brown eyebrows drew together in a frown of determination, but the short hair at the back of his neck prickled uncomfortably.

The following morning Captain Bradner called his crew and lowered the waist boat over the side. Twenty oaken kegs tied in a long line, like beads on a bracelet, bobbed gently beside the hull.

Tub Gibbons pulling stroke oar was nearest the stern sheets. He secured one end of the bracelet to the stern post before he sat down on his thwart.

At Captain Bradner's feet lay a Kentucky long rifle, with a beautifully worked walnut stock and a great barrel polished with loving care. From the standing cleat hung a soft leather shot bag and a powder horn intricately carved from a walrus tusk.

The ship did not anchor but merely hove to, then tacked slowly back and forth under light canvas a mile or so off shore. The whaleboat rowed easily through the calm sea, the casks bobbing along behind like ducklings following their mother.

Nat saw that they were entering a cove protected from the roll of the ocean by a barren sand spit. As the bow hit the beach, Buck jumped lightly ashore and pulled it more firmly onto the shingle. Tub stood up to uncleat the towrope, but with a quick gesture Captain Bradner uncleated the line and scooped up his powder horn and shot bag. "Target practice today, Captain?" Tub asked cheerfully.

"No," grunted the captain. "Go get the water." Then he rammed in powder and shot while the men pulled the casks up on the beach and unharnessed them. Tub hoisted one up on his shoulder, and turned toward Nat.

"Let's go," he said. "The spring's about a hundred yards up the hill." Nat, Joe Governo, and Dan Brink followed, each with his cask on his shoulder. Buck hesitated a moment then easily flipped a cask up with each hand and balanced the pair like epaulettes on his broad shoulders.

"You're a boat-steerer, Buck. You don't have to be a work horse," the captain remarked. Buck grinned.

"I like to be strong, Captain," he replied and followed the procession.

At the spring the men knelt quickly in a circle, hands cupped, and drank their fill of the clear, fresh water. They gleefully washed the salt from their hair and faces, laughing and horsing around like schoolboys. Then they began filling the casks. When the first was filled, Tub banged the bung stopper in with a mallet, tipped the cask onto its side, and rolled it downhill to the water's edge.

While the process was going on, Nat kept a sharp eye on Captain Bradner. What he saw did not cheer him up. The captain sat comfortably in the stern sheets for a while, casually aiming his beautiful rifle at target spots that Nat couldn't see. He didn't fire at them. Just aimed. Then he stretched his legs and again began aiming at unknown targets.

Nat and Gibbons were left filling the last cask. They finally flipped it over on its side and stood up to stretch.

As Nat glanced at the boat, his body went rigid and his hair prickled. Captain Bradner was aiming directly at him!

The crack of the gun and the buzzing of the bullet past his ear stunned him, but instinctively he hit the dirt. Tub stood above him calmly.

"Relax," he smiled grimly. "He didn't mean to hit you or he would have. He's motioning us back to the boat."

Shamefaced and shaken, Nat dusted himself off and followed Tub down the hill. As they reached the whale-boat, the rest of the crew gazed curiously at Nat but not a word was spoken. Nat went directly up to Captain Bradner.

This time his knees didn't shake at all. The captain had far exceeded his rights as a captain and Nat knew it. He hadn't been hit, and he had no intention of crawling in fear. He was a man, and he intended to act like a man.

"Captain," he said evenly. "That shot of yours almost hit me. I ducked from surprise — I've never been shot at before — but I won't duck again. And if I were you, I wouldn't try it again." He paused as curiosity pushed at his anger, then asked, "Why did you shoot at me?"

Bradner's finger caressed the trigger of his rifle. His eyes hardened as they had in the square at Talcahuano. "Because I am Captain and because I wanted to," he snapped. Nat kept his eyes firmly on his skipper, saying nothing, waiting for more satisfactory words. Finally they came.

"I'll tell you why," blurted out the captain. "I'll tell you, young fellow, and it's for your own good. That shot was a warning. Remember this, remember it all the time, remember it aboard ship and ashore. I know who you are and of the rumors about your father. I can guess what's on your mind. I bet you've got a scheme cooking. And if you even look as though you're thinking of jumping ship, the next ball can find you right between the eyes. Now pick up your oar."

There was nothing to do except pick up his oar, so Nat did. On the slow pull back to the ship his mind was in turmoil.

How much did the captain know? Had Manuel talked? It seemed unlikely, but his wits were not too sharp and in the quiet hours of a morning watch when men talk rather freely had he let something slip out? Buck? The captain's favorite — whose side was he really on? Nat instantly rejected that thought. Could Tub have heard more than they thought and passed it along, still resenting the licking he took from Nat? And running through it all the recurrent doubt, were the stories about his father only "rumors," seamen's tales told him by a dimwitted "Portagee" and a superstitious Kanaka?

All in all, his "dress rehearsal" had not been a rousing success.

Discouraged, he avoided Manuel for the rest of the day. Every plan Nat could think of seemed doomed to failure.

Chapter
8

ONE BRIGHT DAY the ship stopped outside an atoll while the natives brought fruits and a few fresh vegetables to trade for tobacco. As the canoes left, Buck motioned Nat to follow him.

"Kanakas tol' me," he said in a whisper loud enough to wake up stones, "over on next islands is white man slave . . . on Manihiki . . . he sound like Mr. Goodwin. What you do we do soon. Two weeks maybe too late . . . up Oahu . . . down by ice. We here now."

He bobbed his head up and down, smiled and stalked off.

Nat knew that he must act. As Buck pointed out, they might never come this close again. Still he hesitated to move by himself. If the ship, with Captain Bradner's firearms, demanded the prisoner, they could undoubtedly get him. With just Buck and Nat, it was a gamble. And although Captain Bradner had shown moments of madness, still he was a New Englander and there was a chance that he would help. With his help the rescue stood a far better chance of success. Nat squared his shoulders and started aft to the captain's cabin.

With his first step doubts began to flit about in his head, but he kept on. Down the short ladder, a twist here, and a turn there in the dark passageways. He ducked a low beam as he entered the mate's country and suddenly, his heart pounding, he stood before the narrow oak door. His first knock was scarcely louder than the pounding of his heart. There was no answer.

He waited a minute then knocked harder. The door swung ajar, and he saw Captain Bradner sprawled out on the great sofa which spanned the cabin. His head lay back on one black horsehair arm and one leg rested on the Turkey-red carpet that nearly covered the deck. A single straight-backed chair, surprisingly delicate for shipboard use, and a pine desk fastened to the forward bulkhead completed the sparse furnishings.

The captain wiped the back of one hand across his mouth, still slack from sleeping. He hitched himself to a half-sitting position and snapped his suspenders back onto his shoulders. Even here in the tropics Captain Elisha Bradner of New Bedford always wore suspenders and his undershirt. "Come in, Goodwin." He rubbed his face with both hands to clear the sleep away. He shook his head slowly a few times and was at last awake.

"Well. What is it? Speak up, lad." All the long way from foredeck to after cabin Nat had been going over in his mind what he should say. Now the moment was here, and in a panic he did not know how to begin. He felt the captain's eyes boring into him, curious, wondering. Nat's knees were shaking and his palms clammy. He was acutely and absurdly conscious of a great horsefly buzzing erratically around the cabin, doomed shortly to die.

Suddenly his mind cleared and his nerves came back under control. He had a reason for being here, and he had a job, bigger than his own private likes or dislikes, to do.

"Captain Bradner," he began, looking steadily into the older man's beady eyes. "I'd like your advice, sir."

Captain Bradner nodded assent. His gaze broke away from Nat's and followed the flight of the horsefly. His fingers groped for the flyswatter on the deck near the sofa. Nat continued.

"The natives brought rumors that a white man is held slave on one of the atolls very near here." He paused expecting some reaction from the captain but none came. The man's eyes merely followed the fly, now buzzing in a far corner of the cabin.

"It seems to me that with a show of strength the *Mingo* could get that man free."

"It's possible," admitted the captain. "But there is a risk involved to the ship, for which I am responsible, and to the men, for whom I am also responsible in a way."

Nat started to speak but the captain raised his flyswatter imperiously, as a king might raise his scepter for silence, and kept speaking.

"You have heard today from some natives that a white slave exists on a neighboring atoll. I heard that same story twenty years ago from other natives and have heard it in various spots ever since. Next you'll be hearing the story about a white goddess on a golden throne." He laughed unpleasantly back in his throat.

"Have the stories never been true?" Nat asked quietly.

"Goodwin," Bradner replied bitterly, "the white goddess is always 'seven sleeps' east or west or north or south. There is no dreamland on earth, lad.

"Now the slave is something else again. Slaves these natives all have seen. And they live in daily fear that a neighboring tribe will come a-raiding, and they themselves will end up hog-tied to a pole. This slave story is a little different. The bad fellows with the whiteman slave are always on the neighboring atoll. Now, if you'll think a minute, lad, you can see right through their game. They get the white whalers to raid the next atoll, killing some and scaring the rest of the enemy tribe. No white slave is found, of course, 'cause he wasn't there in the first place. But the enemy tribe now has the hex sign on them 'cause our 'friendly' natives will threaten them with the might of their great white friends for years to come." He shook his head. "It's an old dodge — exciting when you first run into it, but there's no truth in it."

The plausibility of the captain's story disconcerted Nat. He no longer felt sure, as he had a minute ago, that his father or any other white man was on that atoll.

"Let us suppose, Captain, that we did have proof. Could we rescue a man then?"

"Suppose!" snorted the captain. "Let's not play childish games. There is no white man there."

Nat persisted.

"How hard a job would it be?"

The captain's attention was again on the fly buzzing nearer to the big sofa.

"Probably not too hard. These natives aren't great fighters."

"Then it could be done," persisted Nat.

"It could," agreed the captain, still intent on his fly.

"Then can't we take the chance, Captain? This time there may be a man, and he may be my father."

The captain leaped off the sofa and towered over Nat, the flyswatter absurdly menacing in one hand.

"I don't know who you've been listening to, boy. Probably crazy Manuel. It was on this atoll, right here, that your father was killed by the natives. Clubbed on the head with a stone war club."

"Maybe knocked unconscious," Nat burst in.

"No," said Bradner. "I saw the stone club hit. It spattered his brains."

"Then you were that close," Nat said softly. "And you didn't fire that gun you're so proud of." He expected an outburst, even a blow, but it never came.

Without a word the captain returned to his sofa. "No, I didn't fire a shot. But I can put any bullet right where I want it. You know that, Goodwin, don't you?"

"Then you will not attempt any rescue?"

"I've been wasting my breath on you. Just get out." The flyswatter swished once and the buzzing stopped. With his middle finger the captain flipped the dead fly at Nat. "Out."

The interview was over.

Humiliated and bitter, Nat wanted to be alone. Being alone on a hundred-and-twenty-foot ship with thirty companions aboard takes some doing, however. At last he climbed the rigging and offered to relieve Joe Governo

for an hour or so as masthead lookout. Joe agreed grate-
fully, and Nat took his position.

He had to sort out the whirling muddle of thoughts in
his head. What was he going to do? Was he going to jump
ship with Buck and gamble on reaching the next atoll?
Could they then save his father? If they rescued him where
could they go? Back to Captain Bradner — two deserters
and the man Bradner wanted dead? How could they jump
ship? What about Manuel? Was the slave on the next atoll
his father? Was there any white captive there at all? Was
Captain Bradner right after all? Was Manuel wrong? He
remembered the little idol as his mother turned it over
and over in her hands. . . .

A puff of vapor on the water flicked him to attention.
Sure enough there it was again — two foggy spouts rising
in a "V" above the placid blue water of the sea — there,
beyond, another.

"Blooows," he bellowed at the top of his voice as he
made a megaphone of his hands. "Blooows! Thar she blo
. . . oo . . . ows!"

Far below the men tumbled out on the deck and raced
for their boats.

The captain, first on deck, shouted up. "Where away?"

"Two points off the starboard bow. They'll be crossing
our bow, Captain, 'bout a mile ahead."

The cabin boy had scrambled up to relieve him, and
Nat lost no time in hitting the deck.

"Stand by to lower," snapped the captain with a quick
glance around to be sure that everyone was topsides. "Mr.
Murchison, you will be in command of the ship."

"Aye, aye, sir," replied the elderly cooper, long familiar
with the responsibilities of shipkeeper.

"We'll lower four boats. We're long overdue for oil."
Captain Bradner turned to the mates. "We'll hold course
for another half mile then over we go and devil take the
hindmost."

Nat was shaking with excitement. By now he could see
the pod — half a dozen monstrous sperm whales. Even the
most experienced members of the crew shared his excitement, for this was the real reason that most of them put
up with the hardships of whaling.

This was the hunt, and they were the hunters. Alone,
each was a puny little creature, living constantly pitted
against the great forces of weather and the sea. Put six
in a whaleboat and they could challenge and overcome the
world's largest animal — twice as long as the boat they
rowed, seventy tons in weight, with a toothed twenty-five-
foot jaw and a flat tail that could wipe out a man as
quickly as a flyswatter dispatches a fly.

The helmsman alone, standing aft at the steering oar,
could see the quarry. And tension built up so high, as the
men rowed blindly into battle, that occasionally a green
hand, overcome by the tension in his own mind, leaped
from his thwart into the sea.

As the boats cleared the ship, Captain Bradner sang
out, "A pound of tobacco to the boat that strikes iron first!"
And the race was on.

Unlike many officers, Captain Bradner did not exhort
his crew with a continuous pep talk. He kept the stroke
short and quite rapid compared to the long sweep commonly used, but his boat stayed well under control and
had less trouble than most in choppy seas. As they raced
across the water, his eye checked once again to be sure
the line was coming cleanly from the line tub in back of

Gibbons, a turn around the stern post or "loggerhead" beside his right knee, then forward up the middle of the boat to Buck's harpoon in the bow.

The whales were in no hurry and in no time the boats closed with the pod. Leisurely swimming along, rolling like porpoises, sounding casually only to breach soon after, they were just wasting time. For this reason Nat got a good close-up view of a live whale.

First there was a calm spot on the water perhaps thirty yards abeam, then a gray slab, flat as a barn door but bigger, poked up through the water. It was the very end of the sperm whale's head — his nose, his forehead. It broke through the water and started up toward the sky. Ten feet, twenty feet, thirty feet into the air it rose. Nat watched the great jaw, as long as a whaleboat, studded top and bottom with ivory teeth as long as his hand, open and close slowly. The tower of gray hung for a moment against the sky then tumbled forward into a froth of white water. The whale didn't sound, but rested quietly on the surface. The forehead was as square as the corner of an enormous box, scarred with the rips and gashes of a fighting creature's life. Far back in the head, near the corner of the mouth, a little eye glittered black in the great gray fortress of flesh. It was not an eye like a fish's eye but like that of an animal, with comprehension and intelligence shining within it.

The back in a series of great bumps sloped toward the tail, now flat on the water, awash like a waterlogged raft. As Nat watched, the great flukes began to move; first a sort of curling motion gave the immense bulk easy forward motion, then the flukes, black and glistening, rose from the water — still horizontal because a whale's tail is not vertical like a fish's tail — higher and higher and higher until they were above a tall man's reach. The gigantic tail hit the water once with a splash that drenched every man in the boat. The water rose on the broad forehead, the great back rolled slowly forward, the tail again rose into the air, then slipped silently beneath the waves, and the whale was gone.

"He'll be up again in a few minutes," said the captain. "Be ready for him!" They waited, oars poised, until the captain nodded, motioning them forward. A minute or two later he stiffened slightly.

"Up, Buck. Stand by your iron! . . . Easy on your oars . . . oars up. . . . Give it to him!" Nat heard Buck's grunt, the thud of the harpoon firmly planted in the whale. "Stern all! Stern all!" And the double-ended craft shot back so fast that Bradner had to fight for his balance.

"She solid, Buck?"

"Yes, Captain."

The captain let half the tub of line run free with the sounding whale, then as the line slackened he took a few turns around the loggerhead. He clambered forward to be ready for the kill with his double-edged lance. Meanwhile Buck scrambled aft to take the steering oar.

This whale gave them no sleigh ride but surfaced fairly near the boat. The crew pulled in on the line until the boat was up to the whale. Then the captain deftly "found the life" of the whale with a few expert thrusts of his lance.

In its death throes it jerked the little boat this way and that as it zigzagged around in the sea now red with blood. Suddenly it slapped the water an enormous slap with its tail, once, twice, and again while the boat rocked, its gunwales almost under. Then the great whale was dead. And the long job of turning it into oil lay ahead.

The men took a blow. And the captain, looking around the horizon, reported that Providence Santos' boat had also scored, but the others were rowing back empty-handed.

When the ship was alongside and the whale made fast, the cutting stage was rigged over the side. Already the sharks were ringing the ship, ready to take their pirate's percentage out of the carcass.

For many hours Nat was too busy and too tired to think of his problems. He was astonished at the amount of oil which was simply bailed out of the head with an ordinary bucket. The blubber itself came off in great long strips; the strips were cut into "blankets" weighing nearly a ton each, the blankets into smaller "horse pieces," and these in turn sliced into thin "bible leaves."

The brick tryworks amidships were fired up at once with wood, and as soon as the great iron cauldrons were hot, the blubber was tossed in and the "trying" began. As the oil came out of the horse piece, the tried-out blubber was tossed under the kettle — it still contained enough oil to burn briskly, giving heat to render down its successors.

A red glow lit up the ship all through the night and deep into the following day. A billowing cloud of black smoke poured into the southern sky like a sinuous serpent creeping among the stars.

The men, staggering now with fatigue, hacked and cut, hoisted, pulled, sliced, slipped on the greasy decks, ate gobbets of salt horse and chunks of sea biscuit, swilled down tea and tepid water, sank to the deck for quick cat-naps when they could bear no more and were up and at their tasks again within an hour.

At last the final horse piece was passed up from the greasy blubber room, the last skimming of oil scooped into a barrel, the last chitterling of tried-out bible leaves was destroying itself in its own flames.

As the bung was knocked into the last barrel the men started the traditional chant "Five and forty more." Whatever the size of the whale, whalemen always called it out as worth forty-five barrels. Only this time it was "Five and forty . . . five and fifty-five and sixty more . . . five and seventy . . . five and eighty, NINETY BARRELS MORE."

The men sluiced down the ship and each other in half-hearted fashion with salt water, then tumbled into their bunks for eight hours of sleep, utterly exhausted.

Mr. Flanders' nasal twang was their alarm clock. "Blows." He shouted down the hatch. "She bloows. Step lively." And once again the bleary-eyed foremast hands trotted out on the deck.

"It's a single, Mr. Flanders," called Captain Bradner from his post on the bridge. "Lower your boat and take it alone. We'll rest the other men."

"Aye, aye, sir," snapped Flanders, still stung by the fact that Santos had beaten him to a whale the day before. With him went John Smith, the quiet Mainer who spoke of his family so often that he was always called "Pa," Manuel in the bow, Sal Thurston midship, Content Perkins at the tub oar, and big, black Cato Lee, the harpooner.

Nat shouted good luck to Manuel as they lowered away.

Chapter 9

LASHED BY Mr. Flanders' sharp, impatient commands, the five men bent their oars smartly and the light whaleboat shot away from the ship.

As the whale cleared ahead of the ship, the captain changed course to follow. The change involved only a few points on the same tack, so most of the men were free to line the rail and watch the chase. Providence Santos' crew had been told to stand by if another boat were needed. Alex MacDonald, the little Scot who claimed to have second sight, was biting his lower lip and shaking his head sadly.

"It's a bad day," he wailed. "A bad day, indeed. And the Lord be with them."

The long steady stroke called by Mr. Flanders made his slim boat seem like some giant water strider skating across the slick water.

The whale pushed leisurely along on the surface, its flat forehead throwing broad bow waves like a barge. Apparently in pure enjoyment of its own strength, it would occasionally lift its great tail as high as a house and slap the broad flukes against the sea with a crack like lightning · splitting an oak.

As Flanders' boat came closer to the bull whale, the crew left aboard the *Mingo* grew tense with anxiety. Flanders had misjudged the speed of the whale slightly and had to alter course, running parallel and angling in slightly from behind. He pulled alongside, then abruptly shot for the whale, all men pulling stroke to the stroke.

"Get up, Cato, get up," growled Buck beside Nat. "Free dat harpoon quick, boy."

An instant later Flanders signaled; Cato boated his oar and with one graceful movement swung toward the bow, his harpoon at the ready, his tremendous arm poised. To the men on the *Mingo* it looked as though Flanders meant to put the bow right into the leviathan's side. He didn't intend to miss this one. Six feet away he stopped the stroke. At the same instant Cato let go his mighty heave and the oars followed Flanders' shouted "Back all! Back all for your lives! Give him two, Cato." And the giant harpooner sank another shaft deep into the great side.

At the sting the bull surged forward, then sounded, while the line sang out of the bucket and whizzed around the stern post so fast that it began to smoke. Smith scooped sea water against it to keep it from bursting into flame.

Just before the bucket emptied, the line slacked. Quickly Mr. Flanders slipped a few more turns around the post.

"Get ready," he said curtly. "This fellow may run."

And run he did. A hundred yards ahead of them he

broached. Half his great length shot into the air, hung motionless against the sky for a moment, then fell back into the sea with a splash like the launching of a ship.

"Sit down, Cato," said Mr. Flanders in the calm before the storm. "He's a lively one."

And the whale took off. The line grew taut as a fiddle string and the light whaleboat slapped and bounced across the waves in the fastest boat ride known to man.

Exhilarated by the speed and the danger, the men shouted and laughed and young Sal Thurston kept singing over and over again, "This is really living. This is what I call really living. Oh boy, now, ain't this really living!"

The bull finally slowed his great run and abruptly sounded. Mr. Flanders watched the line with real concern, for a bull his size in deep enough water might pull the whaleboat right under. But this old cachalot merely stayed below to think things over. Cato decided that the sounding was about over and put the hatchet, ready in his hand to cut the line if Mr. Flanders ordered it, back in its rack.

Although almost two hours had gone by, the *Mingo* was not far away; the bull had taken his run upwind in great zigs and zags.

At last the whale surfaced, spouted, then lay quietly in sight.

"Scare him again," grunted Buck at Nat's elbow. "That one ain't tired enough yet."

But from the *Mingo* they saw the oar blades flip down into the water, Mr. Flanders scramble forward to use his lance, and Cato come back to the steering oar.

Cautiously the boat slipped forward; Mr. Flanders raised his hand in a gesture for more speed.

"He's going to nose up and give it to him quick," said Providence on Nat's left. "He's a good lance . . . and a brave man."

Three boat lengths from the whale, Flanders suddenly signaled again and the oars stopped, trailing in the water. Suddenly they backed water and Flanders' form, tall in the bow, turned to say something to the men in the boat. As he turned back, he suddenly changed his mind and called for full speed again.

All along deck the men on the *Mingo* grew tense.

"What's he doin'?"

"Kill him or git away. Don't do no thinkin' now, you mate."

"Stand by to lower," snapped the captain.

Nat manned a fall near Santos.

"It's about all over but the tuggin'," Nat remarked cheerily.

"Not quite," said Santos, his jaw muscles taut with strain. "When Flanders stopped, that bull moved ahead. Now his lance may not reach the whale's life very fast. Whalin', when you make up your mind to act, then act. Second chances sometimes don't come."

Flanders' whaleboat was bow onto the whale and his slender lance planted deep in the dark side. As he churned it, twisting, searching, probing for the spot that would extinguish the spark of life, the red blood poured down the side. Suddenly the whale spouted, and the foam was red.

"Guess he's got him," someone said and a relieved chatter of small words rippled across the deck of the *Mingo*.

In the moment of relief the giant flukes went up the bow, too near the mighty muscle, lifted high in the air, and the boat slid astern. Like a giant hand swatting a fly, the broad fluke clapped down and the whaleboat disappeared.

Stunned, the men on the *Mingo* stood searching the surface of the sea.

Santos and his crew, like the professionals they were, were underway almost at once.

Amidst the oars, the tubs, the splintered planks, and floating spars, they found two men alive. And as the freakish god of luck had willed, uninjured. Santos hauled the dazed men aboard and returned them to the *Mingo*.

Cato Lee and Manuel came back, profound in their silence, withdrawn for a time into their own thoughts. And the men honored their silence and welcomed them without words. But Mr. Flanders, the headstrong hard-driving mate, and John Smith, the big stroke oar who always talked about his growing family and his wife waiting halfway round the world, and Content Perkins, on his first cruise, and Sal Thurston were not with them.

Joe Picard's boat went out for the dead whale floating quietly on the calm sea a short distance from the wreckage.

Cutting in began at once because the sharks would gather fast and tear their huge portions out of the whale. Still on deck long after midnight, Nat was dog-tired, covered with grease and grime, and not yet able to comprehend fully that he would never see these men again. In his mind Santos' words kept up a refrain. "When you make up your mind to act, then act."

Chapter
10

T HE TRAGIC ACCIDENT left Nat mulling the unanswerable questions of life and death and the peculiarities of fate. Yet he came no nearer answering them than other boys who grew into men in the centuries before his time. He did not realize that he was becoming a man. Nevertheless he reached a point where the recollections ceased to be accompanied by a thumping heart and jumping pulse. He realized that Santos' clear comment, made before the accident, explained the chain of events that led to the deaths. He came to believe that he must control the direction of his life as well as just live it. He had learned that a man's indecision can have consequences just as positive as the results of his decisions.

Concerning his own problem, Nat's mind was made up. He must act, and act as soon as possible. Until the last drop of oil had trickled into the cask and the ship had been swabbed down, however, there was no time even for honest sleep. Nat's clean-up detail was the last to secure, and he woke late from his slumber of exhaustion. At once he climbed up on deck.

The weather was sunny and very warm, so most of the men were topsides, as they were nearly all the time in the South Seas. When Nat sought Buck out real secrecy was impossible, and silently he prayed that Buck would keep his voice below his usual bellow.

"Buck," he said without preamble, "just listen. Nod your head if you agree with me, but don't say a word. Understand?"

Buck nodded, then grunted a great bellow of agreement. Half the men on the foredeck looked up startled, saw no excitement in the offing, and went back to sleeping, scrimshawing, clothes washing, sunbathing, writing, Bible reading, domino playing, knife sharpening, and daydreaming.

"I heard Captain Bradner say we're going to the island for water tomorrow," Nat began in a low tone. "Do you still think there's a good chance of saving my fa . . . that white man?"

"Yes," boomed out the deep voice. Then Buck nodded. His eyes were following the black triangle of a shark's dorsal fin clearing the pale blue water.

"You bring fishhooks, line, your knife . . ."

Buck interrupted him brusquely.

"I bring what I want. You bring what you want. No share. One get killed, the other need his own stuff."

Nat nodded. "I'll have my stuff with me . . . and Buck, tell no one, not even Manuel."

Buck's sparkling eyes clouded and he frowned. "Is sad. Manuel is good with his knife."

"I know." Nat looked uneasily around but apparently their conversation had attracted no attention. He noted that Tub Gibbons had moved closer, however, and now stood, back to the foremast, whittling a chain from a piece of whalebone. Nat moved Buck a foot or two farther along the rail. It was all he could do.

"It's too risky to get Manuel from a boat not ours. We'll have to move fast once we start. The captain's good with that long gun."

Nat continued talking rapidly. "We'll both get to the spring at the same time, then make our break. If we can stay together, fine. If we can't, we'll meet on the sunset side of that little round hill. Know the one I mean?"

Buck glanced toward the island, nodded, then his eyes were again taken by the triangular fins as the sharks, attracted by the remains of the dead whale, cruised about looking for more.

Close behind a voice startled them. "Plottin' somethin'?"

They whirled about to see Manuel's smiling face at their elbows. Farther away they heard Tub Gibbons chuckle. "The' ain't no secrets aboard a whaler," he laughed, and sauntered off.

"Don't worry," said Manuel. "Even if you was plottin', he couldn't hear that far."

Finally Nat spoke. "Buck and I are going to try to rescue him."

"Not me?" Manuel showed no emotion. His movement was so slick that Nat scarcely noticed it. Then he saw the thin blade glinting in the sun as Manuel ostentatiously pared his nails. "You think I'm too small? Or too dumb?"

"Neither," said Nat, praying that Manuel would understand. "It's just too risky trying to get you off one whale-boat and me an' Buck off another."

"Suppose I didn't go till after you an' Buck got away. Where would I meet you?"

Nat sighed. "West side of that little round hill you can see down the coast from the spring." He put his hand on his little friend's shoulder. "We'd like to have you and that knife, but we can't wait too long. And don't take any big chances."

The three friends stood side by side, elbows on the rail, each gazing out to sea. A towheaded farm boy from New England, a pint-sized Portuguese from the Azores, a dusky brown native from a tiny island in the South Seas. They were worlds apart in every way and separately their lives had little in common. Little except one idea that they shared — the belief that they could, and therefore should, rescue a man the world believed dead. This idea was so important to each of them that without hesitation each would risk his life for it.

To Manuel the rescue attempt meant the one heroic deed in an unheroic existence. He was now to be denied this as life had denied him so many things. He smiled sadly. "I wish you luck anyway, but don't forget me." Quickly he walked away.

Captain Bradner found his position again just before dawn but lay to until daylight made running the reef less dangerous. He had cruised the Tonga Islands many times before and his old log showed him how he had found the passage through the reef.

He read over it just once, to be sure his memory was

correct, then called Buck to his side by the wheel, put a double lookout on the bow, and easily threaded his way into the calm waters behind the barrier.

They dropped the hook, leaving it at short stay, for there was little wind and no current.

As deck preparations got underway for the trip ashore, Nat took a last long look at the ship that had become his home. He loved the wood polished by use and dark with the oil of many whales. He loved the crowded functionalism of the ship's gear and the sense of activity and excitement it conveyed. His eyes swept the snug little spot forwards of the tryworks where he often sat reading, studying, or just relaxing, and a twinge of emotion tugged at his heart. Now he was leaving this snug world — a floating world that kept him safe from storms, a world with companions whom he admired and who, he felt, liked him.

In the next hour all this world would be behind him. He prayed that it would not be the end of his whaling. He desperately wanted to be a whaler. Would he ever get started toward his goal again? The call to man the boats snapped him back to action.

The captain's whaleboat went over the side. The water casks splashed into the water and were tied together again in their great chain.

As far as Nat could see, Buck was not nervous at all. In fact, he was so completely matter-of-fact that Nat wondered uneasily whether he had forgotten all about the plan.

Buck had his usual place in the bow, and Tub Gibbons pulled stroke. Standing easily by the steering oar, Captain Bradner surveyed the beach, looking for the right

spot to land. At his feet was the beautiful Kentucky rifle
that Nat had come to hate. Whenever they swung forward
for the next stroke, Nat caught a glimpse of it over Joe
Governo's swinging shoulder. And each time the business
end of it looked bigger and closer. It pointed right at Nat.
He felt the short hair at the back of his neck begin to
rise, his mouth suddenly went dry, and his heart began
to pound. Within a minute the sensation passed, however,
and when the bow grounded, he was steady-nerved and
clearheaded.

He thought of simply reaching back, chucking the
rifle into the water, then running, but he was not sure
that one of the other men in the crew, out of the long tra-
dition of supporting the captain, might not simply grab
him or clout him with whatever came quickest to hand.
Tub Gibbons was watching him particularly closely, Nat
felt. And he noticed that Tub had not left his seat. He
was staying pretty close to the captain.

His only choice was to act as naturally as he could. He
hitched up his trousers to be sure his small seaman's pouch
of essentials was hidden, then stepped over the side into
the warm water of the still lagoon.

The line of casks was pulled up on the shingle. Nat
slung one onto his shoulder and started for the thin waterfall that tumbled down the dark mountainside into a deep
pool of pure water. From the pool a shallow brooklet shat-
tered on down to the lagoon. The hillside was extremely
steep, the shell of an old volcano rising about two thousand
feet above the water. To the left a beautiful little valley
threaded its way between the large volcano with its cliffs
and a steep little hill. The fertile floor of the valley was
covered with underbrush and dotted with palms sending

their naked boles and absurd topknots high into the air.

Beyond the cliffs lay the rounded outline of the hill that was their rendezvous. Reaching it by racing up the little valley would be an easy matter, but it would make pursuit easy too. Nat decided that his course would be to run to his right, spiraling around the old volcano, then down on the far side and to the hill from behind.

Nat and Buck reached the pool with Joe Governo and Dan Brink, and Nat signaled Buck to let the other two fill first. Tub Gibbons, Nat noted uneasily, was still back in the boat near the captain, fussing with the stroke thole pins as though something were wrong with them — or as though he wanted to be alone with Captain Bradner.

Joe and Brink filled their casks in silence, bunged them, and started the trek downhill. Nat bent over the pool as though working.

"When they pass that big rock that looks like a thumb, then we go."

Buck nodded. "We meet tonight. Mebbe next time sun get up. You be there." He jerked his head toward the lower trail. "Past the rock. Go now." He took a few steps toward the little valley and disappeared into the brush.

Nat glanced quickly at the whaleboat. To his consternation he saw the Kentucky rifle ready in the captain's hands. Suddenly Tub Gibbons stood up and jostled the captain off balance. Tub waved once before the captain clubbed him with the gun butt. Nat took off. He ran to the right across a sparsely grown patch on the hillside, took a last glance at the whaleboat with Tub lying across the gunwale, then plunged into the thicket.

Captain Bradner was on his way up the hill at once, hunting to kill.

The best course would be around and slightly upward, Nat decided. He wanted the advantage of giving his enemy an uphill chase, for he was sure his legs were stronger than the captain's. On the steep slope of the hill the underbrush was rather thick and gave good cover, and Nat found that he could scramble through it pretty fast. Under his feet loose rocks and clods of earth slowed him down, however, and he could only hope that the captain would have the same difficulty.

He ran in this slipping, sliding fashion until he had to stop for breath. Over the pounding of his blood in his own ears, he could hear below him the labored sound of the captain following his trail. This made him look back, and he saw to his disgust that he was leaving a trail as plain as a horse drawing a wheelless wagon.

Above and to his right a little plateau was gentle enough in slope so that he could cross it with care and leave little trace. To reach it, however, he first had to traverse a bare spot of perhaps fifty yards where he would be totally exposed to anyone below.

He hesitated for a second, heard the captain crashing along, then stepped into the clear space. The ground was so steep here that he turned in toward the hillside and, after a few steps, began to use both hands and feet to get a better hold.

He was almost across when he heard a shout. "Goodwin." It was the captain's hoarse voice. "I've got ye. Quit now or I'll shoot."

His heart up in his throat, his eyes nearly blinded with his own sweat, his fingers bloody under the nails from the little flints in the bank, Nat paused to look down.

The captain was so close that Nat could see his chest

heaving from the steep climb. He could also see that gun — and this time no Tub to knock it aside. But he was aware of his own fatigue too, and decided that the captain's aim wouldn't be steady. Considering the certain choice of a yardarm or the less likely choice of a rifle ball, he took off as fast as he could go for the remaining fifteen yards.

Before he heard the gun's boom, Nat felt the sting. The bullet caught the tip of his left ear and blood began to mix with the sweat on his back. His first thought was "Now I'm safe," for he knew loading the rifle would take so long that he could make the plateau and be off into the forest.

A string of salty curses from below made him turn. Captain Bradner brandished his cherished rifle in frustration and rage and slammed it to the ground. Nat went on his way.

He decided that he could alter his original plan slightly and forego the dubious pleasure of climbing on up the mountain in the tropical heat. He struck off straight across the plateau toward the west. As a farm boy he noticed at once the rich black loam of the virgin forest and marveled at the gigantic green and red leaves of the plants springing out of it. Up here there were no palms, but a smooth-barked tree with thin leaves seemed to spread a pungent odor through the air.

The initial numbness of the bullet wound wore off rapidly, and his ear began to throb painfully. Soon the insects, bad enough before, began to buzz around the clotting blood, and he could not keep them off. At last in desperation he put some of the strong-smelling leaves against his ear, then bound it to his head with his kerchief.

He rested, for pursuit had stopped. The insects seemed to dislike the leaves and Nat had a certain relief though the throbbing pain stayed with him.

Abruptly the trees stopped and Nat was gazing directly into the sky. At his feet a cliff dropped sheer into the valley three hundred feet below. To his left the cliff curved backward toward the sea, to his right it ended in a cleft cut deeply into the volcano's side as though by a giant's axe. Since he could not go straight down and would not go back where he might be seen from the ship, he turned right, toward the cleft, hoping to find some fissure which would make his descent easier. As he walked along, he stayed close to the rim of the cliff. A cool breeze following the contour of the cliff kept the insects away. As there was no longer any need for haste, he moved slowly and his sweat-soaked shirt dried rapidly in the morning air. The sides of the rocky fissure proved to be steep but so split and jagged that climbing down would be no harder than climbing down a high ladder. At the end of the gorge another little mountain stream splashed cheerfully over the edge in a delicate waterfall. Nat thought there might be a place to bathe and to clean up his ear before he went along, and he paused beside a great boulder to look for a good spot. Quickly his eye went up and down the falls. His heart thumped, and his gaze jumped back to a spot ten feet below the top. Nearly hidden in the shade sat a man . . . a white man . . . with a gun. It was Captain Bradner. Waiting.

The captain knew the island and had figured out where Nat was likely to try to descend. He went directly there. And now he was ready.

Nat's first impulse was to backtrack. Then he got behind his own boulder and began to think. Of the means of escape, Captain Bradner had one covered. Undoubtedly word had gone back to the ship and the captain would have Mr. Picard and a couple of other hunters ashore by now. One would cover the beach. Someone else the cliff face. And the other way out was up and over the shoulder of the volcano and down the opposite side. This would take hours and held the risk of exposing him on bare spots.

And if I do nothing, Nat mused, what then? His hunters could not beat the jungle for him. And they would return to the ship before darkness set in. Then he could make his rendezvous with Buck at twilight or in the early morning hours. He sat down in a spot concealed from all angles with a peephole through which he could watch the captain.

The minutes began to drag along. The sense of excitement vanished and was replaced by aching muscles and growing thirst. His exertions in the hot sun had dehydrated him, and the thirst grew worse and worse. Every look at the captain seated by the cool water made it more intense. By midafternoon his tongue felt thick and his mouth cottony, and he began to daydream of wild, impossible schemes to get that water.

His dreams were broken by the sound of voices beginning to climb up the far side of the little ravine. Apparently his pursuers had given up their posts and intended to change plans with the captain's approval.

Then Nat conceived a plan of his own. He reached out for a fair-sized chunk of rock. As the voices reached the halfway point in their ascent toward the captain, he heaved the rock below and behind them toward the bottom of the ravine. It hit with a thump and rolled noisily for a few feet before stopping in the brush. The voices ceased. Nat heaved another rock farther down. Then another and another and another in rapid succession.

"Down there," shouted the captain. "Behind you!"

"We've got him now," came back Picard's voice. "He'll never get away." The captain started down the trail after them. Nat moved over toward the edge of the captain's old seat and slipped into the jungle behind it to wait. Soon the reaction he had expected came.

"Rocks," called out a voice. "Just rocks."

"They must have been thrown from above. Look up there by that rockslide."

Tensely Nat heard the pounding feet approach him as they hurried on up the hill. He held his hiding place until the last man had crossed the stream less than ten feet in front of him. Then he stepped out into the open behind the hunting party, leaped across the stream, and disappeared down the trail they had just climbed.

Buck was waiting at the back of the hill when Nat finally arrived.

Chapter
11

WITH THE SLEEPY unmusical croak of the first bird, Buck's eyes opened. He grabbed Nat's big toe and squeezed it. Nat waked instantly. They sat quietly for a moment in the predawn darkness. The first bird's croak had sprouted into a raucous song of complaint. Other birds, more melodious, happier perhaps at the coming of day, were joining the chorus.

To the east across the open sea the sky turned pale gray then bone white. Streaks of gold began to spotlight random clouds in the eastern half of the sky.

Gingerly, Nat felt his ear. His fingers, cramped from his uncomfortable sleep and raw from scrambling across the hill, told him little. Buck saw the movement.

"Top part ain't there," he said and indicated with his fingers about a quarter of an inch.

"Well," said Nat, "I suppose I'd rather lose an ear than a skull."

"Maybe lose both," Buck said cheerily. To him life and death were all one. He had no fear at all of the future, simply calm acceptance. Nat's imagination was more vivid, and he didn't want it stimulated right now.

"Let's go," said Nat, reaching for his few belongings. "We've got a lot to do today."

Buck grinned and led the way down the hill without a word. In less than an hour they had reached the pebbly beach on the far side that Buck remembered. The palm trees behind them cast long purple shadows into the water. The sun was scarcely above the horizon, the waves not yet awake to any morning breeze.

Three or four miles away several other islands jutted crudely into the sky, some of them were craggy, rugged volcanic islets. To the southwest a different mass lay on the horizon, a flat green-black tar blob low to the sea, with a peculiar shine in the morning sky above it — an atoll.

"How many islands are there?" Nat asked in wonder.

Buck held up five fingers. "More," he said simply.

Nat held up his ten fingers. "Still more?"

Buck nodded gravely, unable to cope with higher mathematics. "Always more. Is many, many, many." A great thought struck him. "Like people in New Bedford. How many?"

Nat nodded, willing to drop his census. "Which one is ours? Where do we go?"

"See little boy?" Buck pointed to the coral atoll. "See big boy?" he indicated a volcanic cone to the right of the atoll. "In back of big boy, Kaneroa. Not far."

Each seemed to know what must be done first — they

needed a canoe, and a large log, fortunately left high
on the beach by a long-gone wave, became the main hull.
While Buck shaped it roughly to give the semblance of
a canoe, Nat disappeared into the underbrush in search
of a second, smaller log to make an outrigger.

Soon they had their crude canoe ready for its voyage.
The big log, sixteen feet long and about a foot and a half in
diameter, had been hollowed out to afford kneeling room,
and the outside planed off into a boat-shaped hull.

At the bow and stern, saplings lashed crosswise ex-
tended four feet beyond the gunwale, then bent sharply
downward toward the water where they were lashed to
the six-inch pandanus log which served as the outrigger.

Buck fashioned two paddles, long and thin but nicely
balanced, with incredibly smooth handles. Into the blade
of each he carved a little symbol, a rough outline of the
same little god that Manuel had brought to Mrs. Goodwin. When he had finished, he placed a paddle upright
on each side of the bow. He signaled to Nat to be silent,
then knelt down on the sand, closed his eyes, and in a low
monotone began to chant a prayer.

Nat's strict Christian upbringing rebelled at this sign
of idol worship, but he reflected that his friend had a right
to worship in his own way provided he didn't insist on
Nat's joining him.

While Buck was still praying, Nat was startled by a great
porpoise suddenly breaking water close to shore then
slowly rolling out to sea again, heading north of the island
that hid their destination.

Buck smiled happily and rose to his feet.

"Tane will help us," he said confidently. "No bad luck. Jus' bad men."

"Only a village full of them," agreed Nat wryly. "Not a worry in the world."

He stepped into the space between the canoe and the outrigger and motioned Buck to join him. "Let's go while luck is still with us."

They heaved the canoe up to shoulder level easily and walked unflinchingly across the pebbled beach. Their feet, calloused from days on hot decks and rough work in the rigging, were by now as tough as shoes. Both wore knee-length faded blue trousers with belts intricately woven from marline during the tedious hours aboard. Buck never wore a shirt; Nat wasn't sure that he even owned one. But Nat had worn a short-sleeved cotton shirt anticipating hours in the insect-ridden undergrowth. Each had a small seaman's pouch strapped to his belt — the only real hindrance to their swimming.

Buck walked right out into the water until it was waist deep. Nat braced himself for the chilly first step or two but the shallow water was merely cool. His feet sank softly into the oozy bottom and the muck came up between his toes. Here and there the roundness of a snail rubbed hard against his skin, but he knew what it was so he paid no heed.

They set the canoe gently down on the water, sat on the gunwale, then swung their legs over the side. They were afloat. Buck dug his thin blade into the water and his shoulder muscles came to life under his glistening skin.

"Wait a minute, Buck." Nat sat with his paddle across his knees. "How far beyond Big Boy is the island we want?"

Buck held up two fingers horizontally indicating half an hour's travel of the sun through the sky.

"Anybody live on Big Boy?"

"No people."

"We'll paddle from here to Big Boy, land, and wait until sundown. Then we'll go on."

"I know," Buck nodded sagely as though he had known for some time.

They bent to the task before them; propelled by smooth rhythmic strokes the canoe made good time toward their destination. The distance was long, however, and the sun hot. They'd paddle for a while then rest a bit. And twice they went over the side to cool off in the water.

There was no reason to hurry, for they must not reach Kaneroa before dark. Food was no problem; both Buck and Nat had slipped good-sized chunks of ship's biscuit into their pouches. Besides, at their first stop both shellfish and swimming fish would be easy to get, and fruit undoubtedly abundant.

They had little reason to fear being seen by the *Mingo* even if Captain Bradner did decide to sail around the island in pursuit. All they would have to do would be to slip into the water on the side away from the *Mingo* and all any lookout would see, unless the ship happened to strike a course within yards of them, would be a log floating placidly on the water. But Nat was sure that the *Mingo* wouldn't even weigh anchor.

By midafternoon they were approaching the volcanic island. Nat started for the south shore but Buck shook his head.

"Tane's porpoise said other side." Nat's New England conscience bridled a bit at being pushed around by a heathen god's pet porpoise, but he could think of no good argument for defending his choice of the south side. So the north side it was. As they approached the beach, they again saw the porpoise, accompanied now by two friends, gamboling in the water ahead of them. Buck's joy was great indeed, and Nat had to admit that the sight cheered him a bit too.

As they slipped by on the north side of the jutting headland, Buck pointed silently to the south. A native fishing party of five canoes was leaving the beach. In a second they were hidden by the land mass. Sensing Nat's thought, Buck said confidently, "They didn't see us. Tane blinded their eyes with happy fishing." Nat prayed he was right.

The reef was riddled with little passages and the log drew only a few inches of water, so their way through the wall of coral was easy. As soon as they beached, Nat insisted that they hide the outrigger in the brush above the beachline, although Buck thought this was unnecessary work, because Tane was protecting it. He helped anyway, tacitly acknowledging that Nat was the leader.

They found a coconut palm with many young coconuts. Following Buck's directions, Nat tied a circlet of rope loosely around the tree, like a fat man's belt on a thin man. With his hands he grasped the bole of the tree as high up as he could comfortably reach, then hooked his toes onto the saggy belt and stood on the rope. It easily held his weight, and he carefully straightened his legs until he was standing on the rope. Again he grasped the tree trunk slightly above his head, held on tight and with his toes raised the loose rope up the tree trunk then stood on it again. In short order he was tossing the young coconuts down from the top of the tree. With his heavy seaman's knife and a sharp stake Buck later opened them easily.

They found clams and a variety of mussels by looking on the underside of rocks in the shallow water.

Since they felt fairly safe from men, either whaler or native, they agreed that a fire would be safe. Nevertheless they built it under the palms so that the fronds, high above, would break up any smoke and knock down any embers floating toward the sky.

Nat's tinder was kept dry in a waterproof bag. He took a small pinch, then struck his flint against the steel, caught a spark in the tinder, and blew softly until it grew to a hot-orange mass that suddenly burst into flame.

When they had finished their meal of fruit and fish — far better food then they were accustomed to — Nat unfolded his plan for the rescue.

"Tonight we will land and hide our outrigger. We will move close to the village. You say it is two or three huts wide and along the coast. You hide near the sunrise end. I will hide by the sunset end. We will watch until people lie down for their naps when the sun is overhead. Then we will meet and make more plans when we know more."

Buck nodded and added, "Take bits of fish in leaves. If dogs find you, give bits. Then they don't bark." Nat made Buck repeat the plan to be sure that there was no misunderstanding. Satisfied at last that there was no more he could do at present, he scrambled up the bank, found a shady spot, curled up and went to sleep.

He awoke about an hour before sundown. He found Buck seated by the bow of their outrigger carving a design into the wood. "It needs eyes," he explained. "It is good-luck boat, Tane says." He stepped back to appraise his own handiwork, nodded with satisfaction, and slipped his sheath knife back into his belt.

Twilight deepened into the blackness of night while they were on the water. Above them stars came, first one by one and then by battalions. Before the low lying atoll was lost in the night, Nat, now an experienced sailor, had chosen his guide star.

The slim paddles dipped quietly into the smooth water, the stroke marked by gurgles and little whirlpools of darkness in the flashing phosphorescence of the Pacific; the recovery marked only by driplets of water from the blade, each bursting into a radiance of sparkles as it returned to the living sea.

Nat thought of the flat island waiting in the darkness. What did it hold for him? Reunion with the father he had not seen for years? Another white man? Or no one at all except savages? His own captivity? Death? For a moment he recalled with horror the stories he had heard of savage tortures. Quickly he shrugged them away. He was doing what he had to do. And he was determined to succeed.

Carefully they threaded their way through the submerged coral, bumping occasionally and twice being forced to turn back and attempt a new passage. At length they reached the relative safety of the lagoon. Quickly they hid the outrigger and marked the spot by walking from the hiding place directly toward the water then turning right and pacing off fifty yards. At this spot Nat placed a good-sized rock — not so big that it would attract attention, nor so small that it would be impossible to find.

"We'll stay here until just before daylight, then hide by the village." Nat flicked an insect off the back of his

FIRST VOYAGE OUT

neck. There was little chance of any native casually
roaming around either in the jungle or on the beach at
this time of night, so Nat judged they could talk freely.

"Tell me as much as you can about these people and this
village," he said to Buck.

Buck told him that these people were not like his
own people, but for generations they had known each
other. These people had darker skin and frizzy hair and
may have been intermixed with a group of Fiji Islanders.
They also had some of the fierceness of the Fijians. In
other respects they were much like their Polynesian
neighbors.

They lived in unfortified villages, because war was not
made against villages but only formally against other warriors. And their houses were round-ended structures of
piling with great low-eaved roofs of thatch. The floors
supported by the pilings were some two feet above the
ground. In the old days, Buck related, custom was to
bring good luck to a new house by burying a man-slave
alive under the end post so that his spirit would always
serve that house. He was not sure whether the custom was
still practiced.

The warriors carried spears which they used for thrust-
ing, seldom for throwing, and war clubs with stone or
wooden heads. A few men had wooden swords edged
with shark's teeth.

Somewhere in the village there would be a larger hut
kept as a meetinghouse which was taboo except on days
of the *fono*, or tribal meeting. Buck was not sure whether
an outsider caught in the taboo hut would be under the
protection of the gods while there or whether he would

be judged guilty of desecrating the temple and given a particularly exquisite and lingering death.

Each of the huts housed a family group with grandfather and grandmother and their married sons. A few yards of scrubby underbrush separated each hut from its neighbor. On the sand Buck drew a sweeping, flattened horseshoe to show the shape of the village. The central part was where virtually all activity took place.

"Very good hunter," Buck continued. "Good with poking spears. Not so good fishermen." He added, with a tinge of local pride, "My place much better with boats, and at swimming."

They talked a while longer in low tones which could not carry far against the whisper of the wind in the palms and the swish of the wavelets against the coral sand. The thought of tomorrow kept neither one awake, for they were used to going to sleep with the ever-present thought that the dangerous chase of a great whale might be their tomorrow.

Then they slept in the way so many sailors sleep, simply by lying down in the most convenient spot and telling their subconscious minds when to wake them. Both fell asleep instantly and waked in the first gray light of morning. They rose quickly and quietly and moved along the high edge of the shore, where the coarse dry sand would not show their footprints, until they could see the first hut of Kaneroa. Then they slipped into the jungle.

Nat took a position at one side of the horseshoe across from the *fono* hut so he could watch the comings and goings of the men. Buck was on the far side where he could see the beach.

The great risk was not that they would be deliberately

sought out, but that some stray glance of a woman going about her tasks, or of boys and girls playing, might happen to light on a peering, unfamiliar face. The dogs were no problem Buck had insisted. They were fat and lazy, and kept for the cooking pot. Besides Nat had his scraps of fish to pacify them in case of need.

Nat crossed a little stream at his edge of town and crawled over the gnarled and twisted roots of a Mape tree which grew on the far bank. He skirted a bamboo thicket then slipped into the growth of giant ferns which came close to the village.

Directly across from the *fono* hut a circular spot about ten feet in diameter had been beaten out in the fern. The growth on the village side was lush and close to the ground. A first-rate peephole looked out onto the village. With a grin at his good fortune, Nat sat down to wait and watch.

As he sat there thinking, uneasiness swept over him. This spot was too perfect. Someone who wanted to spy on the *fono* had made it. Not too long ago someone had cleared this space. He leaned forward to examine the peephole. Sure enough, the fronds had been carefully broken off by human hands. Suppose the someone came back.

The natives were already stirring within the huts, ready to come out to enjoy the cool refreshing air before the tropical sun began to bake the earth. To Nat's right the bamboo thicket offered superb cover. But the canes grew so thickly together that he would have no way of cutting them and removing the evidence before the village came to life.

He turned toward the ferns on his left. Here, too, the

growth was luxuriant, and within three or four yards of the room he left, he found a concealed spot large enough to squirm into. Behind him lay a great log rotting away and covered with green moss. No one would ever come upon him unsuspecting from behind. Carefully he began to enlarge his nest and to prepare a good peephole at ground level and another at sitting height so that he could change his position during the long day. Then he daubed his face and the backs of his hands with black earth in an effort to camouflage himself.

The skin at the back of his neck prickled suddenly. He heard soft footfalls nearby. They passed beyond the log, turned left, and entered the "room" he had just left. Then there was silence. Cautiously Nat parted the ferns on his right and peered through. At first he could make out nothing. Little by little his eyes pieced together a human form nearly hidden by the fronds. It moved forward a bit to look through the peephole and Nat saw with surprise that his neighbor was a girl.

Chapter
12

Small boys were the first up. They tumbled out of each house as though on signal and trudged off all in the same direction — chattering, gesticulating, and shoving one another in sheer joy of being alive. They quickly passed beyond Nat's view. He suspected they were off to the beach on whatever projects seemed important to them at the time.

The older people straggled out by ones and twos. They tugged their breechcloths and shirts more or less straight, scratched their heads through their great masses of fuzzy hair, rubbed their faces, and were ready for another day. Nat chuckled at the number of them who took a quick glance at the sun to be sure it was really there, then promptly sneezed. This was how he reacted mornings whenever he first stuck his head out of the forecastle.

The layout of the village was extremely simple. An

open area twenty yards wide ran straight back from the beach for perhaps a hundred yards. Huts lined both sides of this main street which ran from the shore and ended abruptly in the jungle. Three quarters of the way up the south side of the street was the *fono*, the men's ceremonial lodge, nearly ten times as big as any hut he could see. Toward the shore he saw the masts of four sailing canoes, but the hulls were out of sight below a rise.

Since he could not see the chief's hut, he assumed that it must be on his side of the street and toward the water.

His surveillance of the whole village took only a few minutes. There was no sign of any slave, and the natives in the open area were either doing routine tasks or just sitting in the sun. His mind conjured up a few potential plans of action, but he didn't take the planning seriously, because he didn't know where his father was. He didn't know where the chief was, either, or his fighting men. And there was nothing he could do except sit still and wait.

His attention shifted to the girl, and he cautiously parted the bushes to see if she was still there. She too was patiently waiting, her attention on the big ceremonial hut.

Unlike the villagers, this girl's hair was straight and black, her features more like Buck's. She wore her cloth wraparound neatly and gave Nat the impression that she was a sensitive intelligent person, very different from most of the savages of this village. What had brought her here? What was she looking for?

She was about Nat's age, he guessed. Perhaps she, too, was intent on rescuing someone. Certainly she didn't want to be seen by the villagers. It was not likely that a girl would be advance scout for any interisland war party. And she had no weapon beyond the straight slim knife carried by fishermen.

Whatever her reason for being there, she was certainly a brave one, Nat thought with admiration.

His thoughts were interrupted by the sound of a drum. He returned to his peephole just in time to watch a strange procession come into view. First came a fantastically fat man. He wore a circlet of feathers below his right knee and a feather headdress. Bouncing up and down on his gross belly with every flatfooted step was a long cylindrical drum. Every time he hit the drum he took a step, and the group behind did likewise.

Following the drummer came a score of fighting men. They carried spears about seven feet long, each sharpened to a point and fire hardened. They would penetrate human flesh effortlessly, Nat decided with a quick shudder. The chief waddled in the middle of the group, and just behind him came two miserable-looking brown-skinned slaves. The procession halted in front of the *fono*. The chief took up his position with his face toward the water and the *fono* on his right hand. The fat man motioned with his drum stick and one slave crouched into position as a living stool while the other stood behind to support the chief's back.

The fat man made a short speech to the idol in front of the *fono*, then banged his drum in a rapid flutter. Four fighting men entered the *fono* and came out with a man between them.

Nat's body went rigid and beads of sweat sprang out on his forehead. The prisoner's long hair was blond turning gray, his skin that of a tropics-tanned white man. Was it his father? Nat was not sure. He thought of his father as a younger man, more erect, more alert. The grave face turned slightly and Nat got a better look. He was still not sure, and he felt ashamed because he was not sure. The man turned face on and Nat saw a remembered thin scar high on the forehead . . . then he noticed a quizzical lift to the left eyebrow . . . and recognition flowed through him. It was his father, all right. And Nat's long doubts about the wisdom of leaving his mother alone, journeying halfway around the world, and deserting his ship were over.

His father's face was older, of course, than Nat remembered and showed lines of age and worry. But his body was firm and well fed. The great shoulders and biceps which Nat had poked and admired as a boy were still impressive. He was treated with deference by his captors, as though he were a particularly valuable possession. Nat also noticed that behind his back his arms were ingeniously secured with a cord above the elbows so that he had limited use of his hands. His back and one thigh showed scars that gave testimony to the fact that in the past he had been both speared and lashed — perhaps because of an attempted escape.

His father was escorted to a spot facing the chief, at a distance of twenty paces, and forced to kneel. A guard stood on each side of him and the other two re-entered the dark doorway of the lodge.

They reappeared with another prisoner, this one bound tightly both hand and foot, and threw him roughly to the ground in front of the grinning chief. They undid his bonds and promptly spread-eagled him with wrists and ankles bound to quickly driven stakes.

The chief rose ponderously with the slave behind hoisting him to his feet. Imperiously he beckoned for a spear and approached the prisoner, who was defenseless on the ground. In a deep bass voice he spoke to the prisoner, evidently asking a question. The man replied only in a monosyllable. The chief repeated his question several times with rising anger, finally gesticulating toward the stranger's boat on the shore, then toward the jungle. Nat guessed he was asking who came with the man and where they were. The prisoner talked, but the words were not the answers the chief wanted.

In frustration the chief raised his spear high above the man's stomach. He's bluffing, thought Nat. No one would kill so helpless a man.

Then the girl beside Nat screamed. She burst from her hiding place, raced across the opening, and threw herself across the chest of the prisoner to protect him from the spear.

The warriors promptly seized the girl and held her fast. The chief, laughing loudly all the while, kept threatening her with a spear, but she did not flinch even when he pricked her skin. For a few minutes the arena was full of excited talk and jumping, jostling men, and Nat was unable to decide whether they were telling the girl she would be killed, eaten, or kept as a slave. But she showed no sign of fear, and the warriors soon *tied her* to the man on the ground.

Nat considered moving before the savages came over to see if there were more strangers hiding with the girl. Then his cooler self took charge, and he knew that he must not move at all. The savages were not *likely* to enter the jungle. They always followed trails or pathways instead of blundering through undergrowth, and any awkward movement might give him away. As two fighting men came over to peer cautiously into the girl's hiding place, he slipped down under his great log and lay still. The men poked around for a few minutes with the butts of their spears, then rejoined the group.

Nat immediately returned to his peephole. He counted twenty savages. Of these the chief and the fat drummer would not be fighters. Five looked well past their prime and probably not anxious to fight with anyone. Of the remaining thirteen, half a dozen looked tough. Better odds than we'd hoped, Nat summed up, only three for Buck and three for me.

In less than half an hour the council meeting was over. Most of the men were dozing in laziness and boredom while the chief and his drummer talked on and on. At last Mr. Goodwin was taken back inside, and the savages drifted off toward shady spots in groups of twos and threes. The captive man and girl were left tied to stakes in the sun. For the time at least, they were of no further concern to their captors.

How these two might affect his own plans bothered Nat. Certainly they complicated matters. Cold New England common sense told him that the main job was to rescue his father, and that nothing should interfere if it might endanger their escape. But his New England conscience told him that you don't leave a man and a girl helpless in the hands of cannibals. He began to rethink his plans.

Some time later he heard a hiss repeated at intervals of a few seconds—the sort of sound that wouldn't carry more than a few yards. Nat cautiously shifted position and reconnoitered, head close to the ground. He saw a muscular brown forearm with a whale tattooed from wrist to elbow. He returned the hiss and Buck eased himself over the great log and down beside Nat in the hideout.

"I know ever'ting," he announced. "Ever'ting over there." Quickly he reported his information. The sailing canoe on the beach was from an island near Buck's home. It was very fast and seaworthy — far better than that of these Kaneroans. They had captured the man and girl while fishing, and the girl had escaped into the jungle.

"What will they do with them?"

"Good eating," said Buck. He shrugged off the whole incident. He reported that the strangers' canoe was about three feet above the water's edge. The Kaneroans had two war canoes at the inland edge of the beach and "some" fishing canoes at the water's edge.

The back of the *fono* had a small opening. The chief's hut was where Nat thought it was. The children and some of the women had gone off up the beach and had not returned. Buck thought they were gathering berries or shellfish and would be gone for a long time.

"Run out," Buck concluded, "scare the fighting men. Get Mr. Goodwin, disappear." Nat smiled at the simplicity of Buck's mind and glowed with gratitude for his courage. As Buck talked, however, Nat had been developing his own plan. It was dangerous, but it could succeed. "Now listen carefully," he said. "This is what we'll do." Buck nodded gravely.

"You and I will go to the beach and be seen. The fighting men will come after us and we will run into the jungle. Make them follow us and make noise. When we get near the back of the *fono*, I will hide and you keep going, shouting so they will follow you all the way on around

the chief's house. I will get my father, then we will free
those two and run to the fast canoe. You will come down
the beach as soon as you can. We must fight them off
there and get out on the water."

"Will work," Buck agreed. "But when we go to beach
first pull canoe closer to water. Will be easier." Then he
added, "When you free my people say these words."
And in his native tongue he taught Nat to say "In Tane's
name come with me." Nat repeated the words softly as
Buck nodded.

"If I do not get there," Buck added, "sail to Pole Star.
Do not stop to save me."

A rush of emotion engulfed Nat, for he thought then of
what a great friend he had found in Buck — a pagan
"savage" who had nothing to gain and his life to lose by
offering a lonely boy his help. "Why did you come with
me, Buck?" he blurted out.

Simple Buck thought he was asking a straightforward
question and in surprise gave him an answer. "Because
Mr. Goodwin is a good man. He need you an' me."

"Let's go," muttered Nat and slapped Buck lightly on
the back.

Quickly they worked their way around the village and
reached the beach. They broke cover and ran for the sailing canoe. One on each side of the slim craft they heaved
it toward the water.

"It's rigged," grunted Buck. "That's good."

In the midday heat the somnolent village came to life
slowly, and they had the canoe halfway into the water
before the savages were aroused. Buck leaped quickly
into the canoe, set the sail, and clewed the halyard.

"Now she's ready to sail with one, two big push more."

"We're away," snapped Nat, and they raced back toward the cover of the jungle. The savages had grouped now. Brandishing their spears they came after them with wild shouts.

Nat and Buck started inland on a path twenty yards behind the huts, and the Kaneroans came whooping after them. When Nat judged that he was almost behind the *fono,* he called to Buck.

"Make noise. Lead them away. See you later."

Buck waved and plunged into the undergrowth. In a second Nat heard him give his native war cry followed shortly by an imitation of Nat's voice. Nat lay beneath the ferns until the sound of the pursuers was safely beyond him, then made at once for the *fono.* He loosened his sheath knife in case a guard had been posted, then he tumbled into the hut through the back opening. He landed directly on an outstretched man. Quick as a cat he was on his feet, his knife in his hand. Still half-blind in the dark interior, he reckoned now was no time for subtlety. "Father," he yelled. "Father, it's Nat. Where are you?"

"Nat? Nat who? . . . What do you want?" his father's voice sounded sleepy.

"We've come to get you . . . hurry . . . I'm your son, Nat Goodwin."

His father struggled to his feet still trying to shake off his drowsiness and to comprehend the situation. "Well for goodness sake," he finally said. "I'm awake now . . . my wrists are tied . . . right here."

Quickly Nat sliced the ropes. "We're going out the front door. Then we cut the other prisoners loose and run for their canoe on the beach. Stay close to me."

"I'm with you," said his father grimly. "Let's not waste time."

They burst through the door and out to the stakes. As he cut the ropes on the prisoners, Nat repeated the native words Buck had taught him. Surprised, the man and the girl looked up at him and broke into a babble of native talk. Nat shook his head and said in English, "No understand." The man nodded, and Nat waved toward the canoe. They raced through the shouting women and children toward the beach.

By the time they reached the beach the village hue and cry had brought back most of the fighting men. The sailing canoe was not yet free from the sand as the enemy closed in. Warily the savages faced the little party, unwilling to close with the giant whose strength they respected and the broad-shouldered boy who handled his steel blade as though he knew how to use it. For a moment the battle hung fire. Then three young warriors grunted for elbow room to heave their spears.

One shaft went between Nat and his father and stuck quivering in the log canoe. Nat dodged the one coming at him, then quick as a cat grabbed it as it sailed by. The third glanced off Mr. Goodwin's leg. It drew blood and a great shout rose from the enemy.

"It's nothing," said Mr. Goodwin. "I've got the spear. Watch out, Nat. They'll close now."

Nat raised his arm and flung his spear directly into the mass grouping for a charge. A piercing scream shook the natives' courage as one warrior fell, transfixed by his own spear.

"We can't hold 'em off, boy, and sail the boat too."

"We've got reinforcements coming. Buck's up the beach."

"Buck! Is he with you? There he is now. Well I'll be. . . . How many others?"

"Just Buck. He's all we need, Dad."

"He's got three fleas of his own right now," his father observed. "They might keep him busy for some time."

"Perhaps," said Nat. "But she's still going according to plan. I'll hold onto these spears — each man back of them will think twice before he charges." He made a throwing motion, and the savages backed off a pace or two. "You and our friend here float the hull. Put the girl in the boat. Buck'll be with us as soon as he can."

Buck ran lightly along the beach until he was a hundred feet from Nat's attackers. He hesitated as though frightened, turned sharply to his left and dove into the sea, swimming straight out from land. His three pursuers dropped their spears and plunged in after him.

One of the savages began to pull ahead of his companions, drawing closer to Buck who acted as though he were tiring. Suddenly Buck dove under, and the leading savage stopped swimming to find out which way his quarry was dodging. He found out. Catching him by the legs, Buck yanked him under. In a few seconds his lifeless body bobbed back to the surface. With a yell, Buck started for the other two; in desperate panic they turned back toward the shore — no match for the superb Polynesian in a water fight.

Buck swam easily, rested for a few slow strokes, then disappeared again beneath the surface. Meanwhile the girl had moved forward to get more weight up in the bow to help the boat float free. On the way she gathered the sheet, ready to trim sail at the earliest possible moment.

"Stand by the stern, Dad," Nat called. "Buck'll be at the bow in a minute. You get 'er launched. I'll fight 'em off." He sheathed his knife and picked up the other spear in his left hand.

With a splash and a shout Buck broke water right by the bow.

"Yo, Buck! Heave!" shouted Mr. Goodwin almost lifting the craft by himself.

"Yo, heave ho!" yelled Buck grinning back, then let out a tremendous war cry as he clambered over the bow.

The sailing canoe slid quickly into the water, with the sail up and the sheet now in Buck's capable hand.

"Come, boy," he yelled. "We go now." And then the savages charged. Calmly Nat flung his second spear and a man fell in the front rank. Quickly he shifted the third spear to his right hand and brandished it, but the gang didn't slow up. He hurled it at the leading savage and leaped onto the stern of the moving canoe. Clawing hands grabbed at him as the canoe gathered way slowly into the onshore breeze. The rigging creaked ponderously as Buck hauled in on the sheet, trying to get away on the port tack.

Nat's knife came out again and he slashed at grasping knuckles.

"Dear God," he prayed. "Don't let us drift to leeward." The Kaneroans caught the outrigger beyond Nat's reach. Instantly the man they had rescued leaped onto it, Buck's knife in his hand. The Kaneroans were forced to let go, but a chance spear thrust cut deeply into the man's side, and he was bleeding badly when they helped him back into the main hull.

The sandy shore came ominously close, and a few of the less venturesome savages trotted along the beach waiting for the boat to be blown aground. The wedge of water slowly widened between the boat and the shore, and at last they were free. The savages yelled a hoot or two and began to grow smaller in the distance. A sail finally loomed inshore as they organized a pursuit, but Buck gave it scarcely a glance.

"Like jellyfish chasing shark." He patted the hull. "This kind sail. I know 'em like my own." He changed his course directly for the main opening in the barrier reef.

"Thank you, Buck," said Mr. Goodwin with deep feeling.

"No trouble," grinned Buck.

"Thank you, Nat," said Mr. Goodwin looking proudly at his grown son.

"You're welcome, sir," Nat grinned back happily. "I'm sorry I had to disturb your nap." And that was about as much emotion as any of them ever showed.

They sailed smartly through the cut and out into the open sea.

To where?

Chapter
13

THEY HELD their course for a long run straight out from shore. Buck had the helm and was obviously pleased with his vessel. A type new to Nat, it was not a dugout made from a single log, but a slender ship nearly thirty feet long with a hull of many shaped breadfruit planks sewn together with coconut-fiber cord. It looked rather like the crazy quilt on his bed back in Rhode Island, but the hull was sturdy and the sides formed smooth and true. Because the wood had swollen in the water, the seams were watertight, and the hull so strong that no ribs were needed in its construction. The decorative bow rose proudly four or five feet into the air. The hull itself sloped finely back, like the hull of a racing shell, and tended to lift the light ship above any except very rough seas. Five thwarts were the seats and the only stiffeners used.

Almost amidships the single mast carried a vertical

sprit sail, loose-footed. It seemed a strange, floppy rig to Nat, but it served its purpose well in everything except tacking. The sail was made of a coconut-fiber cloth much stiffer and coarser than burlap.

Buck steered with a long oar in the water on the same side as his sail. Mr. Goodwin sat amidships. Lania, the girl, and her uncle, Kahanu, were forward where she was trying to make the wounded man comfortable. As soon as they were clear of the natives, Nat offered his shirt for a bandage, but she shyly refused it with a "No. You need," in English. Both Lania and Kahanu had learned enough English to talk with the crews of the whaling ships that stopped at their island for water and fresh fruit and vegetables. Lania tore a strip from the hem of her sarong and bound the wound as neatly as she could.

Nat sat entirely outboard of the hull. The outrigger housing made of six long poles crossed with smaller sticks at six-inch intervals supported a comfortable platform, and the crewman's weight counterbalanced the pull of the sail, keeping the slim canoe on a nearly even keel.

In the bow was a fish net, a few yards of coconut-fiber rope, and a fish spear with a three-pronged point made by simply splitting the end of a stick into three pieces, ramming a stone up into the split, and binding it tight. Each of the prongs was then sharpened, notched, and hardened by fire.

On setting out for the day's fishing, Lania and her uncle had taken a jug of water. Under the fish net they found the jug still about half full. This was the entire store of supplies. Nat shrugged and put his mind on other matters.

"Which way should we sail, Buck?" he asked.

Buck pointed northeast. "There," he said. "My island not far."

"How far?"

"Over there. One, two miles. One, two days. One, two weeks. Not so far like New Bedford."

"Good," said Nat wryly. "That cheers me up a lot."

"Buck may not know how to count, Nat," Mr. Goodwin said, "but he'll get us to his island. You can count on that. I used to think it was some instinct like a homing pigeon's, but I learned from a friend on Fatuiva that it's a lot easier to understand. They simply know the ocean around here. They know the fish and where different kinds prefer to be, and where the sea birds prefer to nest. They know the drift of the currents and can read the leaves and sticks and feathers and seaweed carried by the currents and blown by the winds. And they know the Pole Star so they can find latitude."

"What do they do for water?" Nat cut in.

"It rains," said Buck simply. "Chew juicy fish. Drink coconut milk. Sometimes we die."

"If you're giving me a choice," Nat grimaced, "I'll take the rain. There isn't much water and no coconuts aboard."

His father mirrored his concern for a moment, but Buck simply turned his full attention to the sail, confident that Tane would not let them die.

Day passed softly into night with the wind holding steady, and the little craft didn't even change course as she bore steadily northeast. When the stars came out, brilliant in the black tropical sky, Buck found Polaris and altered their course very slightly toward the north then curled up in the bottom of the boat and immediately was sound asleep.

In the still of the night, men at sea have always talked freely. Some age-old bond draws them into brotherhood when they can no longer see the differences of face or shape or color which separate them. The minds, grouped together in the darkness, have a common receptivity which permits fragile thoughts to take shape and sensitive words to be uttered and understood. It was then that father and son finally began to talk of home, of Mrs. Goodwin alone waiting for them there, of the sturdy little house and the potato patch, and the granite boulder in the back yard beside the well where Nat used to perch to watch his father work.

Now for the first time, Nat learned the true story of his father's capture and enslavement. His anger rose when he heard how Mr. Goodwin had found that Captain Bradner was reporting fewer barrels of oil than were filled and was transshipping the extras home with other unscrupulous skippers — robbing both the owners and the crew at the same time.

"I intended to turn him in at the first civilized port. But he guessed that I had learned his secret. When we put ashore for water, the Kaneroans attacked us and Captain Bradner, never a cowardly man, deserted me on the spot. I came to trussed up to a pole, heathen-style. They made it impossible for me to escape, but otherwise didn't treat me too badly. Sort of kept me like a pet . . . oh, once or twice they got a bit playful," he pointed to the intricate network of scars on his back, "but when I didn't holler or flinch, they soon gave that up as no fun.

"You know, lad, if you think hard on the Twenty-third Psalm, you can sort of get your mind apart from your body and tolerate bodily pain."

Nat told his father about the little clay god taken to a barroom in Peru by a Kanaka, and how it had finally reached Little Compton, Rhode Island, half a world away.

"I made quite a few of those," his father nodded. "The Kaneroans traded them to crewmen on various ships. But long ago I gave up any idea that they'd ever bring rescue." He leaned forward in the darkness. "And but for you I guess I'd have spent the rest of my life tied to a stake in a bug-ridden grass dungeon. I know now what President John Adams meant when he said that winning freedom for a man who wants freedom is the highest goal man can have."

While they talked, trading bits of information and comments on this and that, the thread of understanding grew strong between them again and the strangeness engendered by their years apart fell away. Ever since the excitement of the rescue had subsided, Nat had been bothered by a question. His father, he was sure, would want to get back to Little Compton as soon as possible. And two months ago he would have been sure that he would go right back home too. But in these months he had had a taste of the sea. He had learned to enjoy the motion of the ship that had been unpleasant enough to make him sick at first. The creaking of the wood against iron and the strange songs the wind played on the rigging were sounds he loved to hear. The pungent smell of tar, the sweet thick smell of whale oil, and the smell of the sea itself were pleasing to his nostrils. The fierce excitement of pursuing a whale was a long cry from hoeing potatoes. And above all he felt pride in mastering the skills of the craft.

He had learned the knots and splices of marlinespike seamanship in a few days, together with the routine chores of a common seaman's life. Navigation was coming a bit harder because of the mathematics it required, and the finer points of handling a sailing ship lay before him, but he looked forward to learning. He knew he could acquire knowledge of whaling grounds and of the habits of whales.

Hesitantly he mentioned that he thought he might try another cruise if he had the chance.

"I can't blame ye, lad," replied his father soberly. "When I was captive I used to dream of our little place in Rhode Island. But I remember many's the time in Rhode Island, the future looked pretty glum with no cash coming in."

"I figure I'll never get any cash of my own," said Nat. "Unless I get off the farm and earn it. And whaling's as good a way as I know."

"A good man can get up a little fund of his own that way," his father agreed. "And quite a few men are making enough to be rich. I like the idea of your being home with me, lad, but a young man has to make his own life for himself."

While they talked, the wind, which for hours had been steady out of the west, began to haul toward the north. Scudding clouds blotted out the stars, and toward the far horizon the night sky was blacker still with all the stars extinguished there.

"It's not just a squall, Nat, I fear we're in for a real blow."

The creaking mast and slatting sail woke Buck. "Storm," he grunted. "Bad one."

"Heave to on the larboard tack," said Mr. Goodwin. "Let's see which way the wind is veering then. We might as well expect the worst."

Nat promptly came as close to the wind as he could on larboard tack and within a few minutes they found the wind hauling to the right.

"Run with the wind on our port quarter, lad. It's the best we can do. It may be a hurricane, but we're on the safer side. If we have to lie to we'll come over to starboard tack, but this maneuver'll get us a bit farther from the middle of things."

When dawn broke they were still scudding along. The sea was somber gray, and whitecaps chased each other viciously across it. The frail craft bobbed like a cork on top of the ferment. It was difficult to manage with only the steering oar, but the boat stayed fairly dry in spite of the low freeboard. The mast and sail, however, were in trouble. The strain of the wind and the snapping action of the sea was becoming dangerous in spite of the clumsy reef which the three men had taken, using the fish net, during the night.

Kahanu spent a bad night in the bottom of the boat. His side had stopped bleeding but fever had set in. Lania nursed him as well as she could, keeping cool sea water on his forehead and occasionally giving him a sip of water from the jug. There was little, however, that anyone could do except wait and hope.

Finally they decided to heave to on the starboard tack and be content to ride out the storm. The boat was no longer dry, for an occasional comber would fling its crest up, soak the men, and add another quarter inch to the salt water in the bottom.

A single half of a coconut shell was all they had for bailing and they used it steadily hour after hour.

Cramped on his knees in the bottom, totally soaked with

salt spray, chilled by the high wind, his finger stiff from clutching the shell, and his shoulders aching with fatigue, Nat desperately worked on. By midafternoon the three men were exhausted, having worked without food for many hours. Still the storm showed no signs of abating. Although nothing had been carried away, the coconut-fiber ropes used as stays and sheet were fraying badly, with many fibers standing straight out at right angles to the lay. Night came and went and came again and Nat entered a narrow world where he was alone in darkness and peril and pain, his hope of survival ebbing and a sense of doom swelling in his chest.

Delirious now with fever, Kahanu tossed uncomfortably in the bottom of the boat. His condition was much worse, and the flesh around his wound was swelling and turning deep red. Lania kept on nursing him without complaint. Braced uncomfortably athwartships she cradled his head on her lap, stroking his hair softly, trying to get him to sleep.

"I'm sorry there is nothing we can do to help," Nat said to her. And she replied in her soft voice, "Better here than on Kaneroa. Thank you." But the strain was evident in her face and when he was relieved at the tiller by his father, Nat went forward to talk with her, hoping it would take her mind off their troubles for a little while. It gave Nat much pleasure because he had been surrounded by sailors for months and now he could talk, although haltingly, to a pretty girl.

During the night the worst of the storm blew over, as Mr. Goodwin had predicted. The wind stayed high, however, and the seas mountainous. They had no choice but to continue to run before the wind into the fourth day.

In its early hours the storm brought with it the torrential rain of the tropics. Lania filled the water jug by collecting water in the coconut shell. There was no bucket or bag in which they could save more water, however, and the rain which fell into the bottom of the boat promptly mixed with the sea water into brackish bilge.

As soon as Mr. Goodwin thought the mast could bear the strain, the sail was spread and a course set. In the morning Buck spotted the sun's rising point on the horizon, estimated how far the storm had blown them off course, and set his new course more to the northward. Mr. Goodwin nodded approval. Nat fell into the sleep of exhaustion. When he awoke the sun, burning in full fury, was boring into his salt-encrusted skin, his head was throbbing, and his tongue felt coated and thick. His hunger pangs were intense now, and he thought of poor Lania, who had gone a day longer than he without food. She was resting with her eyes closed, her head against the gunwale. Buck was half asleep on the outrigger platform. Mr. Goodwin sat alert and sturdy at the steering oar. He nodded to Nat but didn't speak, and Nat knew that he too must be suffering from hunger pains and close to the point of exhaustion.

When they passed the water jug just before sundown, Nat noticed that Lania did not drink and asked Buck to find out why. There was a rapid conversation and Buck said, "She will not drink the water because there is not enough for us. She says it is ours, all of it."

"Tell her," said Nat, "that she must drink, or else my Christian God will be very angry at us that we did not share alike."

She bowed toward Nat and took a sip of the water, but he thought it was a very small sip indeed.

Night brought relief of a sort, for the sun stopped scorching their skins, but the torture of thirst and hunger did not abate. Buck insisted it was useless to fish so soon on the heels of the hurricane.

The following day brought no relief. They plowed straight across the placid sea until just before noon when the wind died suddenly and completely.

They were becalmed.

The sail hung motionless. The sea became as flat as a mirror, oily on the surface, surprisingly light blue, and dotted with chunks of ribbon weed and kelp churned up by the passage of the storm. Buck tried fishing but nothing disturbed his hook. No birds flew in their sky and no clouds spotted the even blue. No islands broke the tenuous line of the horizon. To Nat time itself seemed suspended — marked only by the throbbing of his own blood in his veins and in his temples.

Kahanu passed from delirium to coma without recovering consciousness and lay now like a corpse with his head still pillowed on Lania's lap.

If the wind had held, they would have made Buck's island in another twenty-four hours. Without wind . . . how long could they hold out? Day again passed into cloudless night. But with the dawn came wind again. They smiled at each other with sun-cracked lips and kept the frail craft plowing its straight furrow across the sea toward their island of salvation.

Although the little craft had been whipped and buffeted through days of storm, it was buoyant enough to ride the waves like a cork.

The rigging was in sorry shape, but it would hold for a few more hours . . . if only this steady and favorable breeze would continue. Except in the months when the trade winds are blowing, however, the wind in the South Seas is a wayward thing indeed. Squalls with and without rain, periods of incredible calm, steady wind, all come and go with a fitfulness that makes prediction only a futile guess. And like the winds of the four days before it, this wind, too, whispered away into nothing and the sea became an undulant mirror of shimmering light.

Each man was sure now, nevertheless, that they would make the island. If an American whaler was in the vicinity, the natives would know about it. If not they would rest and live pleasantly in one of the loveliest spots in the world, eating the delightful Polynesian food, surrounded by friendly people, drinking water — cold water, clear water, the water that falls from rocky streams. All this would be within a day if they were lucky, two perhaps at the most.

They passed into their fifth day in a pitiable state. Keeping lookout at all was a frustrating chore, for there could be nothing to see.

Nat saw something first. A surprisingly large ship loomed suddenly over the horizon on the starboard quarter. It was a good-sized brig coming fast with all sails flying. How long before it would overtake them? Nat's heart thumped with joy as he pointed it out to the others. Then his heart sank.

The brig was the *Mingo Chief.*

Chapter
14

At first sighting, the canoe was ghosting along north-northeasterly with the light and fitful western breeze on the port quarter. She was making headway on the glassy sea, but there was not enough wind to build up any speed.

The *Mingo* lay just forward of the starboard beam and four or five miles away. She had full sail on to take advantage of every little puff, and she was headed northwesterly on an intersecting course.

Squinting through one eye, Nat lined up the *Mingo* over a knot in the starboard outrigger and held his head in steady position for a few minutes. To his dismay the relative position of the two craft did not change, the *Mingo* neither drew ahead of his knot or fell behind it. "We're on a collision course," he muttered. "They're coming right at us."

His father nodded. "We can fall off astern and let her pass by. Or we can change course and make her tack if she wants us. First we'll fall off to see if she really is after us."

Buck nodded, slackened his sheet and altered course.

In a few minutes they saw the mainsail flutter, then fill again on the *Mingo,* and they knew she saw the canoe and intended to talk to its sailors.

Mr. Goodwin's face grew very grave. "We'll have to give back some of the thirsty miles we won yesterday. Come about, Buck, and put her close to the wind on the port tack. If they want us they'll have to work for us. We're two and a half, maybe three miles upwind of them. But this loose-footed, storm-battered log isn't going to windward much better than that squareheaded kettle." He tried to grin, but his puffed lips made a bad job of it. And all of them realized that unless something unforeseen happened there was only one end to this chase — capture. It was a bitter thought.

The *Mingo's* mainsail was spread again promptly, and the familiar hull soon swung around, but not in direct pursuit, as Mr. Goodwin had hoped. She set a course south of that of the canoe which would leave her downwind and in position to intercept if the small craft tried running before the wind to escape.

The great spread of canvas on the whaler and the storm-weakened condition of the canoe and her crew soon made it obvious that escape in the present direction was futile.

"We'll keep changing tack as near into the wind as we can. We can handle faster than the *Mingo.* Perhaps we can make them lose interest." Mr. Goodwin's thirst-parched voice cracked as he spoke. The others nodded in understanding, all knowing that their maneuver would prolong a capture that seemed inevitable.

Nat searched the sky for a bunch of clouds which might indicate a squall or a storm to give them wind enough to get the most speed from their little craft. He knew that under most sailing conditions the canoe could make the whaler look like a tub. And far off on the western horizon was the explosion of clouds which told him a storm was on its way!

For an hour or more the whaler played along after them, weaving from port to starboard tack whenever the lateral distance offered any change of a downwind run. They could make out a figure on deck now with a brassbound telescope glinting in the sun. Captain Bradner knew that his quarry was close and the hunt was in his favor. But the squall on the western horizon was an hour closer.

In the east the sun climbed higher. The heat of the forenoon beat down on the men and the girl in the open boat — the fifth day without food and with little water during that storm.

By noontime they were in sorry shape indeed. And Nat doubted that they could last through the trip to the island even if they were not captured.

About two in the afternoon, Buck squinted and motioned astern. The *Mingo* was lowering two whaleboats. Buck and Nat looked toward Mr. Goodwin. He studied the situation a moment then painfully spoke.

"They'll put one on each side of us and row upwind. They can get us, unless that squall gets here first."

"Why didn't he do that this morning?" Nat asked.

"Just a cat with a mouse."

"There's no way to outrun them?"

His father shook his head. "Work toward the squall and wait for the wind."

"He will kill us." Buck's flat statement ended the conversation.

The whaleboats, manned by well-fed whaling men fresh from a good night's sleep, glided off to either quarter as Mr. Goodwin predicted. Then they began the steady rhythmic chase.

To Nat the slim whaleboats had always seemed things of grace and beauty whenever he watched them from the high deck of the *Mingo*. Now he was getting the whale's view and they seemed like grotesque and odious, little, poisonous bugs striding across the surface of the sea — legs forward on each side, the backward push, then legs forward again. And with each push the bug with its deadly sting was a little nearer. The dark wind squall that could save them hung over the sea just a few miles to the west.

The hunt now moved fast, and the whaleboats were soon within hailing distance. As the danger of capture came closer, Nat noticed that his blood quickened, his vision cleared, and his lethargy dropped from him. In one boat Providence Santos was in the stern sheets and in the other Captain Bradner with his long rifle.

There was only one chance of escape left, and Mr. Goodwin took it. "Come about," he croaked. Then he pointed the canoe downwind between the two boats not one hundred yards away.

Santos was shouting something across the water, but they couldn't make out the words.

Suddenly a loud bang split the air. Nat heard Buck groan and watched him splash into the sea. In an instant

Nat was beside him in the water, holding his face above the surface.

Santos drove his boat toward them at top speed and within a minute or two they were hauled dripping from the water by black Cato and Mr. Santos. Buck was still unconscious; the rifle ball was deeply lodged in his left shoulder.

Captain Bradner easily overtook the yawing canoe with Mr. Goodwin and the girl aboard. During the excitement of the chase, the wounded man had slipped silently from coma into death. Honoring the funeral custom of the natives, Lania placed him in the proper position, then they lashed the steering oar of the storm-wracked craft and left her on the sea to carry her cargo to whatever heaven it might find.

The little procession started back toward the *Mingo.* To Nat it seemed almost as though he had dreamed the dreams of the past few days, that he had never really left the *Mingo* and that this was merely the result of . . . something . . . he didn't know what. He tried to talk, but no words came.

Providence Santos leaned forward. "Do not talk. You must rest first. Now you see only your troubles. But you have many friends."

As they were lifting Buck aboard the *Mingo,* the squall came, too late.

Nat was still in a daze when they reached the deck. He started to stumble past the hatch toward the water barrel forward, but his legs would no longer carry his weight. Two men, he didn't even raise his eyes to see which ones, eased him to the deck and propped him up, back against the hatch, in what little shade there was.

Frenchy DuBois, the cabin boy, held a dipper of water for him to drink, and he grasped it eagerly with both hands. He gulped a few swallows then remembered that he should hold the water in his mouth and he did.

"Take it away!" The captain's sharp voice snapped out and Frenchy stood up slowly with the dipper in his hands. "They'd have had no water for three more days. They'll get none from me."

The crew grumbled and the captain snapped fiercely, "You heard me. They're just three damned deserters! Let 'em rot — until their trial. Then I'll give 'em justice! You bet. Justice. That's what I'll give 'em. But their heavenly island is going to be three days . . ."

He stopped short. Alcide Gautier, the fat French Canadian cook, had casually set a bucketful of fresh water beside the prisoners. He took the dipper from his nephew, ladled it full and held it up to Buck. "Slow," he said. "An' not too much. They's plenny more where dis came from."

Speechless, Captain Bradner stood for ten full seconds in apoplectic rage. Alcide refilled the dipper and held it to Mr. Goodwin.

"Cookie! You heard me. Get up on your feet!" But Alcide kept right on.

"Gautier!" screamed the captain. "Stop giving those men water!"

"Now, Captain," said the cook calmly as he moved back to give Buck more. "You don't really mean somet'ing like t'at. T'ese men t'irsty many days. We haf ta help 'em. Ever'body does."

"I do mean 'somet'ing like that'!"

"I bet you don't truly mean it, Captain. Why, you do a mean t'ing like t'at ever'body New Bedford hear 'bout it.

W'at you t'ink t'en? Eh, Captain? You wouldn't like to walk down de street. No, sir, I bet you."

He spoke to Nat. "T'ats plenny for you now. More you get sick." And he started to pour the rest of the dipper over Nat's head to wash his sweat-streaked, salt-encrusted face.

The dipper went sailing high over the side as the captain's kick struck Gautier's wrist.

"Get on your feet, you pig."

"Yes, sir, Captain."

Cookie scrambled quickly to his feet.

"I said stop giving them water."

"Yes, sir, Captain, I've stopped. I di'n't know you meant it before."

"I meant it."

"Yes, sir, Captain. I b'lieve you."

"Are you going to give them any more?"

"They don't need no more, Captain. But I will if you tell me to."

"Get back to your galley." And he smashed his fist full into the face of the fat little Frenchman.

"Throwing that punch took real courage!" said Alex MacDonald loud enough to be heard.

"Courage!" sneered Murchison, the cooper.

"Aye," said MacDonald loudly. "Would you dare strike the mon wha' can put anythin' inta the pottage that goes inta your belly. He can . . . 'flavour's' the word . . . 'flavour' your every *last* bite."

"Belay that talk." Jim Ward stepped forward. He had been moved up to third mate with Mr. Flanders death. "Captain, shall we resume the regular watches?"

"Yes, Mr. Ward, resume your watches. Put these men

in the brig. There'll be no conversing with them until the deserters are brought to trial." Captain Bradner wheeled and went directly to his cabin. He banged the door tightly shut. Then threw himself on his great horsehair couch both hands pressed against his bursting temples.

Chapter
15

ARCHIE THOMPSON, the carpenter, did the best job he could on Buck's wounded shoulder. Since the death of Mr. Flanders, the tasks of ship's physician had fallen on him. The ball had hit the bone high on the upper arm. It had to be cut out, the wound cleaned, and the arm splinted and bound tight to Buck's chest to prevent his moving it. Throughout the entire process, Buck made no sound nor did his face show any sign of pain.

While the operation was taking place on the foredeck, Manuel brought Nat his own clean clothes. And Jim Ward offered a pair of trousers and a clean shirt for Mr. Goodwin. Except for Cato Lee and Buck, he was the only man aboard with clothes large enough to fit Mr. Goodwin.

Nat had recovered sufficiently to wonder at the thought that less than a week ago he would have found nothing remarkable in getting another pair of trousers from his own sea chest, now it seemed midway between miracle and nightmare. Yesterday was dead, but the future seemed . . . not much of a future.

When they were taken below they found that the crew had padded the hard planks with blankets to make fairly decent beds. Mr. Ward motioned them in. He didn't reach for the irons, and he didn't lock or even close the door.

"They'll be going nowhere, and they'll sleep for hours. Give the poor fellows all the air they can get and let them sleep." Suddenly recalling his new position he said sternly, "And mind you, guard, captain's orders that no one's to talk to these men except the guard. It was a lawful order and within the captain's rights. See that it's obeyed."

"Aye, aye, sir," replied the guard.

It was a needless warning for the three exhausted men and the girl were already asleep. They slept for twelve hours straight with only occasional muttering from Buck, whose fever was rising, to break the sound of their steady breathing.

When at last Nat awoke, he was ravenously hungry and his thirst had returned. Otherwise he felt surprisingly well.

Mr. Goodwin lay asleep, but Buck was sitting up with his back propped against the bulkhead.

"How's it feel?" Nat asked.

"Hurts," said Buck. "He shot."

Nat nodded. Aroused by the noise, the guard poked his head through the door.

It was Limey Bartlett. He glanced curiously at the girl, then at Nat. "You must have quite a story to tell. . . . How be ye?"

"Hungry and thirsty," replied Nat.

"Water ye can 'ave, the captain says. But food 'e says, aboard this ship is only fer workin' men. " He came back with a bucket of water and a dipper. " 'Owever, Cookie says we've been tellin' 'im so long that the mess 'e makes ain't food and only fit fer beasts that we finally convinced 'im. 'E'll be down as soon as the coast is clear. An' yer not to talk to anyone 'cept yer guard. Captain's orders," he added virtuously. "That clear?"

In a little while Cookie came down with a pot of stew and left it with Limey, who refused to let him past "the guard." As Limey passed it in to the prisoners, Nat asked, "How is Tub Gibbons doing? It looked like quite a bash he got back there on the beach."

"It was," Limey agreed. "They brought him back to the ship, but he didn't never come to. Died a couple days later."

"I'm sorry to hear that," Nat said mechanically, stunned because it had never occurred to him that Tub got more than a bump on the head.

"If you was to ask me," Limey said, "I could also tell you your trial is tomorrow morning."

Nat nodded but did not speak, silenced by the weight of his thoughts.

But the trial was not held the next morning. Captain Bradner paid his prisoners a visit instead. There was much that might have been said between them. Nat longed to appeal to the captain as a human being, to ask his pardon for jumping ship, and to point out that his father had been saved as a direct result of his disobedience.

With the forthrightness of youth, he half expected the captain to let bygones be gone and to have things take up more or less where they had left off a week before. During his ordeal he had nearly forgotten the real reason why Captain Bradner had left his father on the island. The conversation was entirely one-sided, however, with Captain Bradner doing all the talking.

"Ye'll not be tried this morning," he began. "Ye've no trip to the Island of the Blessed, or the Damned, today. But there's tomorrow. Oh, yes, there's tomorrow, my buckoboys! And all day today and all night long thereafter to eat on your own livers. And then ye'll have a trial. A fine trial — and right by the tryworks too. And a fair trial. Every bit as fair as the blubber gets when it reaches the tryworks. It knows where it's goin' an' so do you. But Hell's fire is hotter than any tryworks. An' Hell's fire awaits you sinning deserters.

"Shut up!" he snapped as Nat started to speak.

"Say nothing, Nat, lad," his father added in a low tone. "The man's mad."

"Mad! Mad am I," shouted Bradner entering the tiny brig and towering over them. "Tomorrow morning you'll find out who's mad. Before the sun's noon high, we'll have order aboard this ship. Everyone'll know who runs a taut ship . . . a taut ship and a just one. And men who don't obey me don't deserve anything more than justice. And that's what they'll get — justice."

He laughed and slapped his thigh, then ducked out through the low door.

"Let 'em sweat till tomorrow, guard. Let 'em sweat till tomorrow." His voice echoed below decks, and he was gone.

"What do you make of it, Dad?" Nat turned toward his father.

"It doesn't look good for our side, Nat, that's for sure."

His father tried to speak jovially, but the tension in his voice belied his words. "We have nothing to do beyond wait for the morrow. Meanwhile we have food, water, a place to sleep — and some friends."

"What'll happen to Lania?" Nat asked.

"We aren't out of the picture quite yet," countered his father. "But even without us around I think they'd probably drop her at a friendly island. One can't tell for sure with a madman as judge."

"Do not worry 'bout me," Lania said. "No worse than Kaneroans." And incredibly she smiled a warm, touching smile with no hint of worry clouding her features.

"Bless you, girl," Mr. Goodwin smiled back. "And don't you worry either. 'Is no worse than Kaneroans' is right. I'd take my chances here too."

Big Jim Ward, standing on deck at the forward hatch, had heard the captain's words to the prisoners. His uncomplicated mind promptly told him what was right and what was wrong, and his forthright character made him act. He went directly to the captain's quarters.

"Captain," he began simply. "It's not Christian to taunt prisoners. You're Christian and you and your wife go to church with me and mine. I don't believe you should do it again."

Startled by the unexpected words, the captain stared at him. "Furthermore," continued Ward, choosing his words with great deliberation, "the laws of the United States say every man gets a fair trial. Now you're captain and no one can deny it, and you're the judge. But the flag we live under is the United States flag."

"By the Great Horned Spoon," thundered the captain. "Are you lecturing me? You boneskull, you chowder head, you lump of meat. I'll tell *you* the rights of a captain! You'll never have brains enough to be one."

"I know it, Captain," Ward replied firmly. "I ain't smart. But I know right from wrong. It's my Christian duty to be sure that you do too."

"Speak your piece, then get out," snapped the captain, keeping his temper under precarious control.

"Yes," said Jim. "I will. You told those men down there that they were already doomed. And they ain't had any trial yet. They deserve a fair one. Young Goodwin and Buck jumped ship, that's for sure. But Mr. Goodwin — how about him? Some of us might feel that it was *you* deserted *him,* and not the other way round. Here's the rest of it. Nat told you where his father might be. You didn't believe him, you said. But he was right and you was wrong. If you punish him, Captain, back at church people might think you was sinfully wrong. . . ."

"Shut up, Ward, you've finished your piece. Now you listen to me. Them three's deserters. They left my ship and I had to chase 'em down to get 'em again. And I got 'em. Now they'll pay for it. I'm captain of this ship and I'm the one who'll say what trial is fair, if I want a trial, and I'm the one to say what their punishment will be. That's the law, and I run my ship by the law."

Ward turned quietly to the door. "Yes, sir," he said. "You may be right and you may be legal too, Captain. I just wanted to share my doubts with you. An' I ought to tell you now, Captain, I'll share 'em with the congregation when we get back to New Bedford — and with the judge."

The captain's eyes narrowed. "When you get back? No, Mr. Ward, if you get back!"

"If I get back, Captain," Ward repeated, looking Bradner steadily in the eye. "Yes, sir. If I get back." As
he backed out the door, the cabin boy scuttled up the ladder to the deck. Within five minutes the whole ship
knew the story.

But any crew has few individual heroes, and this one
was no exception. Captain Bradner was tough and the men
knew it. He might readily use a belaying pin — or pistol
— on them. He might select them for lashing, or knell-
hauling, or the other punishments of the day. And their
fellow crew members would carry out his orders with
alacrity, even when they didn't agree with his decision.

The thought cooled the bravery of each man, and each
resolved not to stick his own neck into the noose. Yet the
talk now common to the group was that Captain Bradner
was on his last cruise, for his actions, whatever they might
be, would be reported at home. It was agreed that any
punishment for Nat, Buck, and Mr. Goodwin would be
too severe, yet every man aboard knew in his heart that
Bradner would sentence all three to hang at the yardarm
in the morning. And they knew Joe Picard would enjoy
hanging them.

Manuel Bella was most upset of all. He was not born to
be a hero and the stuff of heroes didn't show in him
now. He nervously chewed at his fingernails while he tried
to think. But no plan came to him and the burden he
placed on himself was heavy to bear. He blamed himself
for bringing young Nat from a safe home into this peril.
Yet down below this worry was the deep feeling that he
had done right because Mr. Goodwin was no longer a slave.
What could he do? What now? And the question only ac-
centuated his own indecision. He fingered his slim throw-

ing knife in its sheath, but he knew that he could never kill his captain.

The morning of the trial came. Joe Governo, then on guard, had to wake the four prisoners from their sleep.

"It's the day," he told them softly. "And may God be with you."

"He will be, Joe," said Mr. Goodwin quietly. "Come, Nat, we must face this day like men."

Buck struggled to his feet still weak from his wound. But Nat was fully rested now and had recovered, with the resilience of youth, from his five day ordeal at sea.

A shaft of sunlight slipped down the hatch as the *Mingo* rocked with the gentle swell.

"Bring 'em up, Governor," Picard shouted down. "Captain's waiting for 'em." There was excitement in his voice and, Nat thought, anticipation. Picard was the meanest man Nat had ever known. He was mean with a meanness which was part of him. Even when Captain Bradner was at his worst, the men always spoke of him as sick or mad or crazy. But with Picard it was different. There are some men who enjoy cruelty for its own sake, who get pleasure primarily from inflicting pain, who enjoy watching others suffer. Picard was one of these. Physically small, he was not a pugnacious bully. He liked his victims, like Tony Freitas, spread-eagled in the rigging and tightly tied while he applied the lash. He liked to slip the noose over the neck of the bound victim. He was not a coward, and he didn't avoid danger if it came along. But he didn't enjoy an even fight, he preferred being a torturer. Every man aboard detested him.

Mr. Goodwin was first up the ladder. Then Lania. Then

Buck. And Nat followed, giving the Kanaka what help he could. Governo brought up the rear.

"Over here by the tryworks." The captain's sardonic voice came to them as they blinked in the morning sun. Nat squinted, then sneezed, and was at once alert. The captain stood between the great covered cauldrons, on the brick platform five feet above the deck. He had taken great pains with his personal appearance. His brown beard was neatly trimmed and his hair carefully combed with a part on one side. In spite of the tropic heat he wore a shirt and matching coat and trousers, as though he was about to set out for church back home in New Bedford. Strapped around his best coat, however, was a broad leather belt with two pistols, and at his feet lay his long rifle.

Picard stood on deck a pace or two nearer the crew. He had certainly not prepared himself for the occasion. Naked to the waist, his tanned body showed the dirt of the day before. Greasy trousers cut off just below the knees completed the uniform of this unlikely mate of an honest whaleship. Just in front of one temple a round livid scar showed where once in his past a victim had almost become the victor. And many a man since had wished that he had.

The crew stood, more or less in ranks, along the port side between the mainmast and the tryworks. The starboard deck was clear except for the prisoners and their guard.

"Prisoners, stand at attention," snapped Mr. Picard.

There was not a sound from the crew, but electricity was in the air.

Captain Bradner cleared his throat. "Does any man here

deny that these men, two of them last week, and one before this cruise, were members of the ship's company of
the *Mingo Chief*?"

No one spoke. "That will be written in the log, Mr. Picard. You will also write in the log that myself, Governo,
Brink, and Gibbons witnessed the desertion of young
Goodwin and Buck." There was no sound, no motion from
the crew.

Nat's eyes sought out Manuel Bella. The little man was
standing as far from the captain as he could get, as though
he wished himself a million miles away. The muscles
around his mouth, tightening and relaxing spasmodically,
indicated the great tension he was under, for Manuel believed that all of this was his own doing. He had decided
that Mr. Goodwin was alive. He had brought Nat from the
safety of his home to the *Mingo*. And he had known deep
in his heart that only by defying Captain Bradner could
Nat hope to rescue his father. And now all three of Manuel's friends, including big kindly Buck, would die, because he, Manuel Bella, had done all these things. But Nat
noticed only the outward signs — the nervousness in his
friend's face, the fact that he was dressed in his best
clothes, as if he, too, were ready for church. But low on his
chest swung a leather sheath with a slim throwing knife
cradled in plain view.

"You will further record in the log that myself and
Manuel Bella witnessed the desertion of Mr. Goodwin in
1836. And that these men therefore now stand before me
convicted deserters awaiting just punishment."

Bella's thin high voice shaking with nervousness came
clearly across the deck. "Do not log that for me, Mr. Pi-

card. It is not true. I saw Captain Bradner desert Mr. Goodwin on the beach."

"Then do not log it, Mr. Picard," the captain said with a peculiar half smile. "It would be Bella's word against mine." He laughed out loud. He turned to the prisoners. "Mr. Goodwin, do you choose to evade trial on a technicality or to stand with your son?"

"I'll stand trial with Nat and Buck," replied Mr. Goodwin quietly.

"Then prepare the ropes, Mr. Picard."

"They are ready and the knots tied, Captain," said Mr. Picard eagerly.

Mr. Ward's resonant voice filled the air. "Captain, I told you yesterday that I would expect to see these men brought to fair trial. This is no trial in my opinion."

"Hear, hear," came a chorus of voices from the crew behind him.

"So it's not a fair trial, eh, Mr. Ward . . . Mr. Lawyer Ward," the captain began, as if he could bluff down the mate, but suddenly his manner changed and a crafty look came into his eyes. "But we'll have no one saying I'm not a just man. Fair treatment they'll get, and it's better than they gave me."

He turned to the three. "I picked ye out of the sea when ye had no food, no water, and a leaky craft with a wind-ripped rag for a sail. It's better than ye deserve, but I'll give it back to ye. We've run downwind from your little island, but maybe there's an unknown, uncharted one waiting for you out there." He swung his hand widely from east to west. And he laughed uncontrollably for a long minute.

"Mr. Picard, lower the small staging into the water.

It's the nearest thing we have to a catamaran. There's no mast on it — but then there's no sail either so they won't need a mast. Oars they won't need for there's no place to row to . . . but give 'em a board to paddle with . . . and to fight off sharks."

Manuel Bella broke ranks. He walked steadily across the open deck toward Nat and placed his hand on Nat's shoulder. "My friend," he said. "I got you into this and I don't see no way out. . . ."

"Bella, back where you belong," the captain roared.

"Captain," Providence Santos stepped forward . . . and suddenly the captain had a pistol in each hand.

"Get back at once or I'll shoot!"

Bella glanced proudly at the angry man. "I have always the right to say good-bye to a condemned man. I . . ." The old muzzle loading pistol boomed like a cannon and Manuel toppled sideways with the bullet in his head.

"Don't anybody move," shouted the captain. "I've still got this one ready. Reload, Mr. Picard." He tossed the smoking pistol to the grinning mate. "We may have to kill the whole bloody mess of them before this cruise is over." And then he giggled. There was no doubt about it now. The captain was mad.

Standing beside his dead friend, Nat calculated the chances. Manuel's knife was in plain sight. Could Nat kneel, draw it and throw from his kneeling position with any chance of success? He saw Ward and Santos edge toward the captain. "Stand there, Mr. Ward," ordered the captain, "or you'll join Bella." Nat knew that for trying to protect the Goodwins, Ward was marked for certain death now or later. Quickly he acted.

As Nat dropped to his knee, Captain Bradner wheeled

toward him. As he whipped Bella's knife for the throw, he saw the great pistol aimed directly at him. The knife had left his fingers, and he was falling toward the deck when the boom finally reached his ears. The bullet slammed into the flesh of his left shoulder and spun him around. He hit the deck on his back.

He scrambled to his knees as Mr. Ward reached the captain and laid him gently on the deck, the haft of the knife sticking from his belly. Mr. Picard made a dive for the rifle, but Providence Santos got it first.

"Quiet," he said. "Now we need quiet. Listen. We have all thought this thing might come and hoped it would not. It did. Our captain was took crazy. He needs more doctor's help than we have. I am in command, and we sail at once looking for help. Now we must have no more of this." He held the gun above his head, then tossed it to Cato Lee. "Mr. Ward, take what men you need to get the captain to his cabin. Thompson, you will see first to the captain's wound and then to Goodwin's. Mr. Ward put on all sail. We go to Honolulu."

The *Mingo Chief* once more rolled into normal ship's routine. The blood was washed from her decks, the wounded made as comfortable as possible, and the frail body of Manuel Bella sewn in canvas, weighted, and slipped reverently over the side.

Chapter
16

Nat's wound bothered him considerably, and the fact that he could do nothing useful bothered him more. He was impatient to get on with his work of whaling and a chance to learn enough to rise above the forecastle. Although he drew considerable pleasure from the simple fact of being aboard, he could not stand being in his hot bunk below decks and so made a pallet on the foredeck.

Lania spent much time with him there, teaching him native words, learning English, helping to make pleasant in memorable little ways hours that would have been dull. He saw less of his father, who had offered to stand a mate's watch, but the disturbing thought of parting was often in his mind. Common sense told him that soon both Lania and his father would be gone, and he knew that their departure was right. But in the night his emotions rebelled now and then and flared into colorful dreams which he reluctantly let fade.

Mr. Santos had decided to sail for Honolulu, in the Sandwich Islands, ten days or so away, so that he could report to the shipowners' agents and leave Captain Bradner under proper care. The north-northeast course for Honolulu passed close by the Society Islands, which Buck and Lania called home. The sturdy old *Mingo* was no catamaran, however, and in the scarcely perceptible breeze wallowed slowly on her way.

When the ship finally made a landfall and entered the lovely little harbor, an odd trio stood at the rail — Buck and Nat with their left arms swathed in bandages, the lithe Polynesian girl between them. The girl was talking earnestly to Nat.

"Stay with us," she urged. "Get well here." She waved toward the beautiful island.

"Fine place," added Buck. "Plenty fish, chickens, pigs, fruits, fresh water. You like it." He nodded. " 'Nother ship come soon. Sign you on."

Nat shook his head. "I've signed on for this cruise with the *Mingo,* and I'll stick with it. My arm won't be long a-healing, Thompson says."

"Me, too," Buck agreed. "Stay on *Mingo* with you."

Nat looked down into Lania's dark eyes. "I would like to stay here with you, but I must go. It is my job." Because she was a well-bred Polynesian girl, she knew that she must not argue with a man, and she would not spoil a parting with too much sorrow. She rested her hand lightly on Nat's forearm and said nothing.

When the first native canoe came near, she turned quickly to Nat. "Thank you," she said softly. "Come back some day." Then she cleared the rail, spread her arms in a swan dive, and was gone. She did not board the oncoming canoe but swam alone toward shore without looking back. Later in the day as the ship left the harbor after adding fresh provisions, Lania was in a canoe which conveyed them back to the open sea. She was with a group of young people, laughing, waving gaily up at Nat. He waved back and felt a little tug of envy at his heart, for now she was smiling just as warmly at the boys in her canoe as ever she had smiled at him.

The following morning the *Mingo Chief* was hailed by a whaler riding low in the water. It was the *King Philip* bound for New Bedford with a full cargo.

"Any letters?" came the signal.

"Yes," Mr. Santos signaled back. "And we'd like to come aboard." His boat was lowered, and he and Mr. Goodwin visited the homeward bound ship. An hour later they returned.

"Nat," said Mr. Goodwin without preliminaries of any sort. "Unless you've changed your mind about whaling, I guess this is good-bye. Captain Slocumb will give me a ride home."

Like many big, kindly men, he was awkward at expressing his emotions. Nat was much like him, so they stood silent for a minute or two, trying to find words when words weren't really needed. Finally they used the usual "take care of yourself," "thank you" kind of phrases that men fall back upon. They shook hands, and Mr. Goodwin walked toward the ladder.

"Tell mother I'm all right," said Nat. He glanced at the sweater and extra shirt in Mr. Goodwin's hand — all the baggage he had. "Don't let anyone steal your sea chest."

His father grinned at the little joke, and as the whale-boat pulled away, he waved and called out the time-honored farewell of whaling men, "Greasy Luck!"

With a lump growing in his throat and tears close to his eyes, Nat waved back. He stayed on deck until the two ships had parted and even the bright sails had faded into the distance.

Nat learned his trade well and later became one of the great line of whaling captains who had their own ships before they were twenty-five. He thought often of the strange beginning that had brought him to the sea. Again and again in memory he saw the funny bandy-legged man rolling along the country road while a boy in a potato patch leaned on his hoe watching. And always he thanked God that the boy had believed Manuel Bella's strange story.